DEADLY SUMMER

Elizabeth reached for the receiver. "Hello, newsroom."

"This is a friend calling." The voice was a whisper, strange and sexless.

Elizabeth put her hand over the receiver and whispered loudly, "Seth! Come here!"

Puzzled, Seth walked toward the desk as Elizabeth said, "Can I help you?"

"I wanted to let you know—there is a bomb."

Elizabeth's eyebrows shot up, and she waved to Seth frantically to pick up the extension on the next desk. The caller was Redman. It had to be.

"Where is the bomb?" she repeated so that Seth would know what they were talking about.

Redman's laugh was cheerful, but there was an unmistakable edge of madness in it. "In a place where there are plenty of folks, that's where."

Beside her, Seth was scribbling hastily on a pad. He held the pad out to her: *Keep him on the phone.* When Elizabeth nodded, he hung up and, using another line, dialed a number.

"Where is it?" she coaxed.

"Valley Cinema. But don't worry. It'll go off before you can get there."

Bantam Books in the Sweet Valley High Series
Ask your bookseller for the books you have missed

#1 DOUBLE LOVE
#2 SECRETS
#3 PLAYING WITH FIRE
#4 POWER PLAY
#5 ALL NIGHT LONG
#6 DANGEROUS LOVE
#7 DEAR SISTER
#8 HEARTBREAKER
#9 RACING HEARTS
#10 WRONG KIND OF GIRL
#11 TOO GOOD TO BE TRUE
#12 WHEN LOVE DIES
#13 KIDNAPPED!
#14 DECEPTIONS
#15 PROMISES
#16 RAGS TO RICHES
#17 LOVE LETTERS
#18 HEAD OVER HEELS
#19 SHOWDOWN
#20 CRASH LANDING!
#21 RUNAWAY
#22 TOO MUCH IN LOVE
#23 SAY GOODBYE
#24 MEMORIES
#25 NOWHERE TO RUN
#26 HOSTAGE!
#27 LOVESTRUCK
#28 ALONE IN THE CROWD

#29 BITTER RIVALS
#30 JEALOUS LIES
#31 TAKING SIDES
#32 THE NEW JESSICA
#33 STARTING OVER
#34 FORBIDDEN LOVE
#35 OUT OF CONTROL
#36 LAST CHANCE
#37 RUMORS
#38 LEAVING HOME
#39 SECRET ADMIRER
#40 ON THE EDGE
#41 OUTCAST
#42 CAUGHT IN THE MIDDLE
#43 HARD CHOICES
#44 PRETENSES
#45 FAMILY SECRETS
#46 DECISIONS
#47 TROUBLEMAKER
#48 SLAM BOOK FEVER
#49 PLAYING FOR KEEPS
#50 OUT OF REACH
#51 AGAINST THE ODDS
#52 WHITE LIES
#53 SECOND CHANCE
#54 TWO-BOY WEEKEND
#55 PERFECT SHOT
#56 LOST AT SEA

Super Editions: PERFECT SUMMER
SPECIAL CHRISTMAS
SPRING BREAK
MALIBU SUMMER
WINTER CARNIVAL
SPRING FEVER

Super Thrillers: DOUBLE JEOPARDY
ON THE RUN
NO PLACE TO HIDE
DEADLY SUMMER

SWEET VALLEY HIGH
Super THRILLER

DEADLY SUMMER

Written by
Kate William

Created by
FRANCINE PASCAL

BANTAM BOOKS

NEW YORK · TORONTO · LONDON · SYDNEY · AUCKLAND

RL 6, IL age 12 and up

DEADLY SUMMER
A Bantam Book / July 1989

Sweet Valley High is a registered trademark of Francine Pascal.

Conceived by Francine Pascal

Produced by Daniel Weiss Associates, Inc.,
27 West 20th Street, New York, NY 10011

Cover art by James Mathewuse

ISBN 0-553-28010-4

Published simultaneously in the United States and Canada

Bantam Books are published by Bantam Books, a division of Bantam Doubleday
Dell Publishing Group, Inc. Its trademark, consisting of the words "Bantam
Books" and the portrayal of a rooster, is Registered in U.S. Patent and Trademark
Office and in other countries. Marca Registrada. Bantam Books, 666 Fifth Avenue,
New York, New York 10103.

PRINTED IN THE UNITED STATES OF AMERICA

O   0 9 8 7 6 5 4 3 2 1

DEADLY
SUMMER

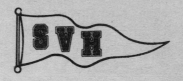

One

"I'm telling you, Liz. It's for real."

Elizabeth Wakefield gave her identical twin sister a teasing grin and put a chicken-salad plate on her tray. "Come on, Jess. You don't really believe all that crazy Ouija board stuff, do you?"

"Then how do you explain it?" Jessica asked as she tossed her sun-kissed blond hair off her shoulders. "It *knew* I'd have a date for the Endless Summer concert."

A laugh bubbled up in Elizabeth's throat. The fact that the Ouija board correctly predicted that Jessica would have a date for the concert wasn't exactly mind-boggling. Pretty, flirtatious Jessica could have had a date for almost every single night of the week. Anyone who knew her could have made the same prediction.

Hiding a smile, Elizabeth pushed her tray along the chrome rails toward the cashier, paid for her lunch, and made her way across the crowded Western Building cafeteria. Jessica followed her. Since she and her twin had begun working as summer interns at the *Sweet Valley News*, they hadn't had leisurely lunch breaks. Usually they grabbed a sandwich whenever they could spare the time, and Mondays were always especially rushed.

But after work, the summer nights seemed to go on forever. Lately Jessica had been spending her evenings with her good friend Lila Fowler. Lila had just returned from London and brought back a Ouija board, which, according to her, was the latest craze in England.

It was typical of Jessica to get caught up in trends. Nearly every month she had a new hobby, dated a new boy, and followed the latest fashion trend. Almost anything new or unusual was sure to be a hit with impulsive, daredevil Jessica.

Elizabeth was at the opposite end of the spectrum. She stayed with one thing until she excelled at it. Her main interests were reading and writing. Working at the local paper for the summer was just another way for her to achieve her goal: Someday, she knew, she would be a professional writer. Even at sixteen she wrote poetry,

2

short stories, and one-act plays. Elizabeth was steady, dependable, and thoughtful—about as different from Jessica as a person could be. There were times when Elizabeth could hardly believe they were even related, let alone identical twins.

But, personalities aside, they *were* absolutely identical. Both had size-six figures, blue-green eyes, and dimpled left cheeks. The summer sun had darkened their golden tans and brought out the highlights in their wavy blond hair. The Wakefield twins were quintessential California girls. Only the fact that Elizabeth always wore a watch and Jessica never did was a giveaway. As their mother often joked, Elizabeth had been born on time, and Jessica, four minutes late.

Naturally it had been Elizabeth's idea for them to spend the summer "chained to newspaper desks," as Jessica liked to say. But her initial objections had evaporated once she had met several handsome reporters at the *Sweet Valley News*.

Not even Elizabeth had expected their summer to be so exciting. Within days of starting their internships, the twins had been caught up in a grisly murder case. When that was wrapped up, mob hit men and a boy in the protective witness program had dragged Elizabeth and Jessica into serious danger.

"Summer's almost over," Elizabeth mused.

3

She swallowed a mouthful of chicken salad and glanced at her sister.

Jessica grimaced. "Don't remind me."

"Oh, come on, Jess. Getting back to school might be pretty relaxing after the summer we've had."

"That's true," Jessica agreed. She popped a grape in her mouth and sighed. "I think I'll ask the Ouija board if I'll have any fun at school this year."

Elizabeth bit back a sarcastic reply. Instead, she rolled her eyes as she said, "You don't need a message from the 'other side' to tell you that, Jess. I can make the prediction now." She dropped her voice a register and said in a thick accent, "Yes, you vill have fun at school zis year."

"Ha-ha. Go ahead and laugh," Jessica retorted. "But I know there are things in this world we can't explain." She gave Elizabeth a pointed look. "UFO's, paranormal disturbances—"

"Para-*what*?" Elizabeth choked on her soda. For a moment she alternated between laughter and coughing. "Jess, come *on*," she scoffed.

"You come on, Liz," Jessica insisted. "You know sometimes we have ESP with each other."

"Yeah, well . . ." Elizabeth's voice trailed off, and she poked her straw into the crushed ice in her cup. It was true that being identical twins

4

often meant they could sense things about each other when they were apart. "But that's nothing like a Ouija board, Jess, and you know it."

Her twin smirked. "You just don't want to believe in anything you can't find a rational explanation—"

"Right," Elizabeth cut in dryly. "I can't find a rational explanation for why you always need to borrow my clothes when you have twice as many as I do and when you like totally different styles, but I sort of doubt there's anything supernatural about it."

"You just don't understand." Jessica lifted her chin and looked away. She added a haughty sniff for emphasis.

Elizabeth shrugged and wiped her fingers with a paper napkin. The rational explanation was that either Lila or Jessica was deliberately—or unconsciously—guiding the answers. What Elizabeth didn't understand was how Jessica could be so gullible about it.

"Let's just forget it, Jess. Anyway, we'd better get back upstairs, or our summer jobs will be over a few weeks early."

At seven o'clock the twins arrived at the Dairi Burger, Sweet Valley's most popular hangout. Within seconds of stepping through the front

5

door, they spotted the table where several of their friends were sitting, waiting for them.

"Liz! Jess! Over here!" Cara Walker waved eagerly as they headed over.

"Hi, y'all," Jessica said with a wide grin. She flopped into a chair next to Lila Fowler and helped herself to a spoonful of Lila's ice cream.

Elizabeth sat down in the corner next to her best friend, Enid Rollins. Enid and Lila didn't like each other very much, but because Lila was Jessica's friend, and Enid was Elizabeth's friend, they often found themselves together when they were out with the twins.

"I got another letter from Jeffrey today," Elizabeth whispered to Enid.

"Geez, when does he have time to be a camp counselor?" her friend teased. "He spends all his time writing to you."

Smiling, Elizabeth pulled the folded sheets out of her bag and smoothed them with a flourish. Her steady boyfriend, Jeffrey French, had been working at a camp near San Francisco all summer. It was difficult not being together, but they talked on the phone at least once a week and wrote each other letters almost every day.

"What's new at camp, anyway?" Enid asked. She pushed her curly brown bangs off her forehead and added, "I bet it's cooler up there than it is down here."

Elizabeth's eyes ran down Jeffrey's letter, and a smile lit up her face. Much of the letter was private, but there were parts she could tell her best friend about.

"He says he might have some great news for me, but he's keeping it a secret. What do you think it could be?"

"I have no idea," Enid replied.

"Well, I don't know why he has to be so mysterious about it. Maybe he's—" Elizabeth broke off as her sister's voice rose at the end of the table.

"Last night Lila and I asked the Ouija board if I would ever be on TV, and it said yes," Jessica announced triumphantly.

Just then Ken Matthews and Winston Egbert came over to the table. Having heard what Jessica said, the two boys exchanged a meaningful look. "Is she serious, or what?" Ken drawled.

"Totally serious," Winston replied. He was the class clown, and he had an answer for every situation. "Ouija boards have predicted the careers of all the major stars, you know." Winston sat down beside Elizabeth, reached for a napkin, and handed it to Jessica. "Can I have your autograph now, Jessica, while you're still an unknown?"

Everyone laughed, including Jessica and Lila.

"You never know, though," Cara pointed out

7

reasonably as Ken Matthews pulled up a chair. "It could just mean you'll be on the news or something, even if it's only for two seconds."

"Trust me, Cara," Jessica replied in an airy tone. She piled her blond hair atop her head and showed her profile. "When I'm on TV, we're talking major celebrity status."

Elizabeth's shoulders shook with silent laughter, and she smiled at Lila. "I don't understand how you can waste your time on something so incredibly silly," she said. "I know Jess can be a space agent, but I thought you were smarter, Lila."

Another roar of laughter met Elizabeth's words, and a blush colored Lila's cheeks.

"Maybe I'm just a stupid idiot with nothing better to do, right?" Lila demanded.

Elizabeth gasped. "I didn't mean—"

"No, forget it. I know what you meant," Lila snapped. She balled up her napkin and tossed it onto the table. Then she stood up and stalked to the counter where people placed their orders.

Elizabeth shook her head. Lila Fowler was one of the richest girls in Sweet Valley and also one of the most insecure. The slightest hint of criticism caused Lila to flare up instantly. A silence fell over the group.

"I didn't think she would take it so personally," Elizabeth spoke up.

"That's our one and only Lila Fowler," Ken said lightly.

Elizabeth sat back and groaned. "Sometimes that girl . . ."

"Don't worry about it," Enid suggested. She cocked her head to one side and shrugged. "You know how she is."

"Yeah, I do, so I shouldn't have said anything."

"Well, anyway—"

"Hello, little children. I have arrived!" a drawling voice cut into the conversation at the table. Arrogant Bruce Patman pulled out a chair and straddled it, adding, "This social occasion can now officially start: Patman is here."

"Big whoop-de-do," Jessica retorted, her voice oozing scorn.

Elizabeth rolled her eyes. If there was one person more spoiled and exasperating than Lila Fowler, it had to be Bruce Patman. He had an ego the size of the Western Hemisphere, Elizabeth thought. In fact, his motto could be summed up by the vanity plates on his black Porsche: 1BRUCE1.

"Hell-o, Bruce," Ken and Winston intoned in singsong unison. They were both Bruce's friends, and they weren't at all intimidated by him.

Bruce grinned and set his tennis racket on the table. Obviously he had just come from the courts. "And the master wins again, thank you very much. Does the phrase *complete and total massacre* mean anything to you kids?"

In their corner Elizabeth and Enid glanced at each other, both repressing their laughter. Bruce was so preposterously conceited, they couldn't believe it sometimes.

"Maybe Jessica can ask the Ouija board if he'll ever win at Wimbledon," Enid suggested in a whisper. "It's worth a shot."

Elizabeth snorted and clamped one hand over her mouth. "At least if it said yes, Jess would have to realize how stupid it is," she muttered, her eyes dancing. Then, glancing at her watch, she sobered up. "Oh, gosh. It's almost eight. I'm baby-sitting for Mrs. Bartel tonight, so I have to go."

Everyone said goodbye. On her way out Elizabeth grinned, just thinking of how she would begin her reply to Jeffrey's letter later on: *Dear Jeffrey, everything is the same in Sweet Valley. Bruce is negotiating for total world domination, and my sister has completely flipped out again.*

Two

Jessica watched silently as Lila came back to the table, soda in hand, and sat down again, a haughty expression on her face.

After a few sips, Lila asked tersely, "Ready?"

Jessica shrugged. "Sure. You want to go?" She was spending the night at Lila's.

"Yes," Lila answered sharply.

Arching her eyebrows, Jessica swallowed the last of her soda and looked at Lila. Obviously her friend was still smarting from Elizabeth's dig about the Ouija board.

"Then let's hit the road," Jessica said in a mild voice, ignoring Lila's irritable scowl.

"Are you guys leaving?" Cara piped up.

Lila gritted her teeth and swung her expensive leather bag over one shoulder. "Yes. We are leaving. We're leaving, everyone," she went

11

on, raising her voice sarcastically. "Everybody got that? Any questions?"

"Not from me," Bruce said.

"Good." Turning, Lila strode away.

Jessica pushed herself up from the table and gave her friends a tiny smile. "Looks like I'm leaving, folks. Bye, y'all."

In her lime green Triumph, Lila shifted gears and raced the engine as they drove toward her home, Fowler Crest. Her father, one of the wealthiest and most extravagant men in Sweet Valley, had built a palatial mansion on the hill overlooking the town. But, as an only child, Lila rattled around inside it like a pea in a barrel. Jessica liked to sleep over, but she suspected that tonight Lila would do nothing but complain.

Scrunched in her corner, Jessica shot Lila a glance as they zoomed around a bend. "What's bugging you, anyway?"

"Nothing."

Jessica grimaced. She knew perfectly well that Lila wanted to be cajoled into talking.

"No, seriously," she urged. "What's wrong?"

As Lila turned her car into the drive, she let out a frustrated sigh. "Your *sister* just acts *so* superior sometimes, I could scream."

"She wasn't cutting you down, Lila."

"Then what do you call it?" Lila demanded as she opened the car door and stepped out. "She practically said I'm stupid."

Jessica rolled her eyes as she got out of the car, but she didn't say anything right away. She knew Elizabeth would never deliberately be insulting.

"Can't you take a joke?" she asked finally.

"Ha-ha. Some joke."

Jessica and Lila walked up the steps to the front door. Inside the cavernous front hall they paused. The house felt empty and was silent.

"My father went to Japan on business," Lila said, as though reading Jessica's mind. "Our housekeeper's probably in her room."

Jessica nodded and followed her friend up the wide, sweeping staircase. Their footsteps were muffled by thick carpeting.

"She really acts like Miss Perfect Know-It-All," Lila stormed on. She looked sharply at Jessica as she opened her bedroom door. "Doesn't she ever tick you off?"

"Well . . ."

Jessica shrugged and crossed the room. She switched on the light. Instantly her reflection blinked back at her from the wall-to-wall mirrors. She opened a drawer, rummaged through the clutter of makeup, and perched on the marble counter. As she unscrewed a bottle of nail polish, she raised her voice. "I guess she does. Sometimes."

13

"Don't you ever want to get back at her?" Lila called from the bedroom. "You know, teach her a lesson?"

Jessica brushed Tropic Flame on one thumbnail. "I don't know. I guess," she muttered, trying to decide if she should paint her nails different colors or all the same.

"There has to be a way to make her take it all back. She's so sarcastic about the Ouija board, and I bet she's never even tried it." Lila appeared in the doorway, her arms folded.

Jessica glanced up. "So?"

"I'm trying to *tell* you." A conspiratorial look crossed Lila's face, and she sat on the edge of the bathtub. "I have a plan."

"Oh, yeah?" Jessica perked up. She wasn't as upset about Elizabeth as Lila was, but she was always ready for a scheme.

"So what do we do?" Jessica prompted. Her eyes sparkled as she looked at her friend. Lila gave her a taunting grin. "Li? Come on. What is it?"

Lila crossed her ankles and said slowly, "What if we can get the board to make predictions that are *guaranteed* to come true?"

"Sure, Lila." Jessica snorted.

She shook her head. Secretly she didn't *really* believe in the Ouija board. Half the time she deliberately pushed the planchette to make answers, and the other half of the time she knew Lila was pushing.

"No, I'm totally serious."

"You're seriously kidding yourself," Jessica scoffed, examining her fingernails. "You'd have to know something that was definitely going to come true," she pointed out. "And not something really obvious, either."

"Give me a little credit, please," Lila said, annoyed. "As a matter of fact, I do know something that no one else knows, and it isn't something obvious."

"Like what?" Jessica lowered her hands and looked intently at her friend. She knew the look on Lila's face.

"You know the Endless Summer concert?"

"Yeah, sure. It's next Saturday. So what about it?"

Shrugging airily, Lila said, "It's going to be postponed for a whole week."

Jessica stared. "How do you know?"

"The guy who's running it is a friend of my father's," Lila explained. "But anyway, what I was thinking—"

"When did you find out?" Jessica cut in.

"Yesterday, but—"

Jessica's voice rose indignantly. "You've known since yesterday, and you didn't tell me?"

"I did tell you. Just now," Lila retorted.

"Yeah, well, thanks a lot for letting me know," Jessica seethed. She shook her head in disbelief. "I would have told you immediately, Lila."

"OK. I'm sorry," Lila huffed. "Geez, you can be so sensitive." Before Jessica could comment, Lila breezed on. "The plan is to get Liz to do the Ouija board with us tomorrow night. We'll do a few easy answers and then lay the concert on her. When she finds out it's true, she'll flip."

Jessica leaned back against the mirror, mulling over Lila's plan. It might just work. At least it would shake Elizabeth up.

"There's a problem, though," she pointed out. Lila cocked one eyebrow, and Jessica went on. "What if everyone knows by tomorrow night?"

Lila rolled her eyes. "If it isn't a secret anymore, then it won't work. *Obviously.*"

"OK, OK." Jessica let her mind run through the possibilities. An impish smile lit her eyes. "I know where she keeps Jeffrey's letters. We could use something really private from them."

"Good," Lila said with a grin. "That's good. Just something to soften her up."

Jessica let out a peal of laughter. "She'll be so surprised. She won't know what to say."

"For once," Lila added.

Their eyes met, and they both giggled. Jessica had to hand it to her friend. If there was anyone who could cook up a plan, it was Lila Fowler.

Elizabeth was loading the dishwasher on Tuesday evening when her twin bounced into the kitchen, grinning.

"What's up?" Elizabeth asked lightly.

"Lila's coming over."

With a sarcastic smile Elizabeth said, "Great."

Jessica took a plate and rinsed it before stacking it in the dishwasher. "I know she's not your favorite person in the world, but she's bringing over the Ouija board, and we want you—"

"No way," Elizabeth cut in. She glanced at her sister from the corner of her eye. Jessica was looking extremely innocent, always a danger sign. "You aren't getting me into one of your dumb séances."

Jessica looked hurt. "But, Liz, why not? I mean, so you don't believe it, but you've never even tried. Give it a chance. Besides," she added slyly, "you're always saying writers should be open to all kinds of new experiences, right?"

"Do I always say that?" Elizabeth teased.

"Yes, you do. Now, come on. It can't hurt. Or are you afraid you'll find out something you don't want to know?"

Elizabeth faced her sister and laughed. She

17

knew her twin was a champion manipulator. "I'm not afraid of anything," she replied.

Jessica folded her arms and leaned back against the kitchen counter, her blue-green eyes twinkling with mischief. "So?" she prompted challengingly. "Aren't you the teeniest bit curious?"

"No."

"You're a terrible liar, Liz."

Elizabeth giggled and flicked water off her fingers at Jessica, who squawked and ducked away. "Well, maybe I am a little bit," Elizabeth confessed. "But *just* to see how you and Lila fake the answers."

"I knew it," Jessica said, ignoring Elizabeth's cynical words. "As soon as Lila gets here, we can start."

Elizabeth rolled her eyes. "I can't wait."

Half an hour later Elizabeth and Lila followed Jessica up to her room. After sweeping a pile of laundry off her rug, Jessica opened up the Ouija board.

"OK, Liz, you sit on this side. Lila, over there, and I'll sit here," Jessica ordered.

Elizabeth did as she was told. Although she didn't want to admit it, she really was curious about what her twin and Lila did during their sessions with the Ouija board.

The Ouija board had an arc of bold block letters stretching from side to side. Elizabeth could see it consisted of the alphabet. At one edge were the words *yes* and *no*.

Lila opened her shoulder bag and took out the planchette, a miniature triangular table with three legs. In the middle of it was a clear plastic circle about the same size as the block letters.

"OK," Jessica began in a hushed voice. "I'll turn off all the lights except one."

Elizabeth grinned and then stage-whispered, "The spirits won't be able to see us."

"Shh," her sister hissed. Jessica turned off the overhead light, but she let the light from the closet stream out into the darkened bedroom.

Lila shot Elizabeth a look of weary patience. "That's just the way we do it," she said.

"Got it." Elizabeth tried not to smile or to make any more snide remarks.

"OK, Liz," Jessica explained. "You put your fingertips on the edge of the planchette. Right," she added as Elizabeth followed her instructions. "Really lightly."

"I'll ask the first question," Lila spoke up. She rested her fingers on the other side of the planchette.

While Elizabeth watched in skeptical silence, Lila closed her eyes. "Is there anyone here the spirits have a message for?"

Nothing happened. Elizabeth ducked her head to hide a grin. It was obvious that Lila and

Jessica were trying to set a mysterious, spooky mood.

"Me?" Lila went on. "Or Jessica?"

The planchette was still motionless, sitting in the middle of the board.

"How about me?" Elizabeth offered.

After a moment's hesitation, the planchette crept across the Ouija board toward the word *yes*.

"What a surprise," she added mildly.

"Cut it out, Liz," Jessica warned. "Can't you try to be serious?"

"Sorry," Elizabeth whispered. She didn't know why Jessica and Lila insisted on acting as if the planchette moved by itself, but she was willing to go along with the game.

Lila cleared her throat. "What is the message for Elizabeth Wakefield?"

The planchette began to inch forward again. Elizabeth moved her arms to keep her fingers in contact with it. She was positive Lila was guiding it. While they watched, the planchette glided back and forth across the alphabet, spelling out *good news*.

"Good news," Jessica repeated in an excited voice. "That's great, Liz. OK. Can you tell us what the good news is?"

Again the planchette swept across the board, picking out letters one by one. "S-E-C-R-E-S," it wrote.

"Must be *secret*," Lila muttered.

Jessica nodded, and looked eagerly at Elizabeth. "That's what it is! You'll get some good news, but it's a secret."

Cocking her head to one side, Elizabeth frowned at the board. Just the day before, Jeffrey had written to say he might have some good news but wasn't going to say what it was. A sneaking suspicion entered her mind, and she glanced sharply at her twin.

"Have you been reading my letters?" she demanded.

Jessica gaped at her. "What? Of course not," she blustered. She looked at Lila in astonishment and then back at Elizabeth. "Liz, I wouldn't do that. I swear."

As Elizabeth met her twin's eyes, she tried to read Jessica's mind. Jessica met her gaze steadily, a faintly injured expression on her face. Reluctantly Elizabeth broke eye contact.

"You believe me, don't you, Liz?" Jessica prompted. "Honest—I wouldn't read your private letters."

"I guess."

"Is it true?" Lila spoke up. She had an I-told-you-so smile on her face. "Are you getting some secret good news?"

Elizabeth shrugged. "I don't really know," she admitted. "I mean, it's kind of vague. Maybe.

21

But that doesn't prove anything," she added hastily as a meaningful look passed between her sister and Lila.

"Liz—"

"It doesn't," she interrupted Jessica. Elizabeth gave them both a lopsided grin. "It's just a coincidence, you guys."

Lila and Jessica shared another look, and Lila nodded. "Maybe it is. Let's ask something else."

As soon as Lila and Elizabeth placed their fingertips on the planchette again, it started moving quickly.

"It must be important," Jessica whispered, her eyes wide. "C-O-N-C-E-R-T," she read off as the planchette picked out the letters. "What about the concert? The Endless Summer concert?"

The planchette quivered, and then traveled to the word *yes*.

"Something about the Endless Summer concert?" Lila breathed in excitement. "OK. What about it?"

"D-E-L-A-Y," the board spelled out.

"Delayed?" Lila echoed. "For how long?"

"W-E-E-K" were the letters that appeared next.

Lila gasped. "Delayed for a week?"

"Y-E-S" was the board's answer.

Elizabeth burst out laughing. "Oh, come on, you guys. That's totally ridiculous. Just this afternoon Seth asked me to check all the details for an article he's running tomorrow about the concert. There's no way it's going to be postponed." She chuckled softly. Seth was one of the reporters at the paper.

"Well . . ." Jessica pursed her lips. "Maybe we misunderstood. Maybe we asked the wrong way."

Elizabeth unfolded her legs and stood up. "Look, you guys, it was fun, but I've had enough."

"But, Liz, you promised!"

"And I did it, OK? I never said I'd spend all night asking questions," she insisted, heading for the door.

Jessica and Lila glanced at each other and shrugged.

Elizabeth chuckled again and headed downstairs. Her twin and Lila had been subtle about it, but she was positive they had been guiding the planchette. What she didn't understand was why they would make such an unlikely prediction. Still grinning, she walked into the kitchen to pour herself a glass of juice. The phone rang as she shut the refrigerator door.

"Hello? Wakefield residence," Elizabeth said into the receiver.

"Hi, this is Seth. Is that Liz or Jessica?"

Elizabeth smiled. "Hi, Seth. It's Liz. What's up?"

"You're never going to believe this. Lawrence just called me." Lawrence Robb was the features editor of the paper. "He just found out the Endless Summer concert is being postponed, so we've got to get in early and rewrite the story."

Elizabeth stared at the juice in her hand. "What?"

"I said, be at the office first thing. We have to make some more phone calls, get quotes from the people involved on why they're delaying—"

"It's being *delayed*?" Elizabeth repeated incredulously.

Seth let out an exasperated sigh. "That's what I'm saying, Liz. So we need to get on it first thing. OK?"

"Sure," she said mechanically.

After hanging up the phone, she turned to stare at the closed kitchen door. Upstairs, Jessica and Lila were probably still asking the Ouija board questions. She didn't want to tell them it had been right about the concert.

But how could that be? she asked herself in confusion. *It can't be a coincidence.* She shook her head to clear it. She knew the Ouija board was all mumbo jumbo.

Or was it?

Three

A fresh breeze from the Pacific was blowing as Elizabeth and Jessica left for the newspaper office on Wednesday morning. Frowning moodily, Elizabeth put the top down on the red Fiat convertible she shared with her twin, then got in. She started the car before Jessica was even seated.

"Hey, wait a second," Jessica yelped. "Don't leave without me."

Elizabeth grimaced. "Oops. Sorry."

"You've been on Mars all morning." Jessica pulled her hair back off her face and glanced at her sister. "What's your problem?"

For a moment Elizabeth hesitated. So far, she hadn't told Jessica what Seth had called about, so she covered her uncertainty by concentrating on backing out of the driveway. She knew Jessica would soon find out that the prediction about the concert had come true, but still, she wasn't sure she wanted to say anything about it. It was too strange.

"Liz?" Jessica was looking at her with a questioning smile on her face.

At last Elizabeth managed a lighthearted laugh. Shaking her head, she said, "You'll never believe this, it's such a coincidence."

Jessica cocked her head. "What?"

"Remember what the Ouija board said about the Endless Summer concert?" Elizabeth said as she drove. She tried to sound unconcerned. "It's true. Isn't that funny? Seth told me last night."

"No!" Jessica gasped, and her blue-green eyes opened wide with surprise. "You're kidding me! That's so incredible!"

"Yeah, well, I guess you and Lila made a pretty good guess."

A tiny frown creased Jessica's forehead. "What do you mean?"

"Come on, Jess. I know the Ouija board doesn't really send messages from a time warp," Elizabeth said. She darted an apprehensive glance at her twin and swallowed. "It was just a lucky guess."

"Liz, even if Lila and I were faking it, *which* we weren't," Jessica added reproachfully, "it's got to be about ten million to one we could guess something like that. I mean, be honest, huh?"

Elizabeth didn't answer. Confused, she tried to concentrate on getting through the busy morning traffic. She knew it was unlikely that Lila and Jessica could have guessed something like that, but what other explanation could there be?

Jessica hitched herself around in the seat to face Elizabeth. "Let's just say, hypothetically, that Lila and I were trying to fake you out. *Something* must have told us what prediction to make, right? So it still comes to the same thing."

"Jessica, this is all totally ridiculous," Elizabeth replied. Her voice was sharper than she meant it to be.

"All I'm saying is, try to accept that there might be something to it, that's all," Jessica huffed.

Elizabeth made a face and turned her car into the tall parking garage adjoining the Western Building. If there was one thing she didn't want, it was to accept that there might be "something to it."

"We could try again tonight," Jessica went on as they headed for the entrance to the paper a few minutes later. "You know, just to see if it was a coincidence."

With a shrug, Elizabeth pushed open the door to the fifth floor. They stepped into the bustling corridor of the *Sweet Valley News*. The soft chatter of computer keyboards and telex machines created background noise for the buzz of conversation. Reporters, typists, and editorial assistants passed back and forth between the offices.

Elizabeth took a deep breath. Everything there was real—reporters used facts and photos. There were no coincidences, no strange, elusive happenings such as Ouija board predictions. It felt reassuring to be where things were written down in black and white.

"Liz?"

She turned to smile at her twin. All she had to do was remember she was a reporter. "Sure, Jess," she said easily. "If you want to do it again tonight, it's fine with me."

"Great. Oh, by the way, did you find your journal yet?"

A flicker of annoyance passed across Elizabeth's face. "No," she said and sighed.

When Elizabeth had gotten ready for bed the previous evening, she discovered that her journal was missing. She remembered having taken it outside to the patio so she could write down some thoughts she'd had during the day. But then her mother had come home and started dinner, the phone had rung, the dog had started barking, and things had gotten a bit hectic. Afterward Elizabeth couldn't recall what she had done with her journal, if she had put it down inside, if she had taken it upstairs, or if she had left it outdoors. A fifteen-minute search had turned up nothing, and after breakfast this morning, there hadn't been time to look again.

Elizabeth shook her head. "I put it some-where," she mused. "Oh, well, it'll turn up."

"Maybe we could ask the Ouija board where it is," Jessica suggested as they headed for their desks. They smiled at two of the secretaries who were talking by the water fountain.

"Yeah, sure." Frowning, Elizabeth pulled out her chair and sat down.

"Hey, Liz! You're here!"

Looking up, Elizabeth saw Seth Miller strid-ing toward her. She tried to put her personal problems aside and think about her job.

"Listen, here's the deal," Seth began as he straddled a chair next to her. "Last night the managers decided to put the concert off for a week—I understand there's a problem with the musicians' union. Anyway . . ."

Elizabeth listened and jotted down notes on a legal pad, but half her attention wandered back to the night before. If the decision to postpone had only been made the previous night, there was no way Jessica or Lila could have known ahead of time. So it was either a wild guess, or else the Ouija board—

"Liz?"

Startled, Elizabeth glanced up at Seth and blushed. "Sorry," she muttered.

"Something the matter?" Seth's serious brown eyes lingered on her for a moment.

"No. I'm just spacing out. Sorry."

Elizabeth forced herself to concentrate on the job ahead. Seth rattled off a list of people for her to call and asked her to get all the information for him before lunch. She nodded firmly, and Seth left, calling out to another reporter.

"What do you have to do?" Jessica asked, peering over her shoulder.

"Make some phone calls about the concert," Elizabeth muttered.

Jessica nodded solemnly. "It's so weird that the Ouija board told us it would be canceled, isn't it?"

"Yeah . . ."

Looking smug, Jessica strolled back to her desk.

For a few minutes Elizabeth sat staring into space. More than anything, she wished Jeffrey were back from camp. He was always so reassuring, so down to earth. She was positive that he would offer a simple, rational explanation for what had happened.

But he wasn't around, and there was no one else Elizabeth felt comfortable confiding in. Usually she could talk to Enid about anything, but Elizabeth was afraid her friend would scoff at her the way they had both scoffed at Lila and Jessica. As much as she hated to admit it, Elizabeth felt strangely fascinated by the Ouija board.

Well, I'll find out tonight if it was just a huge coincidence, she told herself finally, *or if there really is something—someone—communicating through the Ouija board.*

Across the crowded office Jessica sat at her desk, leafing through the Yellow Pages. One of the reporters was doing an article about catering services, and Jessica had to get rental prices on party tents. In Jessica's opinion, it was a menial and boring job.

She slumped in her chair and pouted. Then she caught sight of her sister and bit her lip to keep from grinning. Elizabeth was staring into space.

I know what you're thinking, Jessica told her twin silently. *And that's not the only prediction that'll come true, either.* After dinner, the Ouija board would tell Elizabeth where the missing journal was. Jessica would be prepared to swear on a stack of bibles that she didn't have a hand in it. Before too long, Elizabeth would be a true believer.

By the time she and Elizabeth finally got home, Jessica was extremely impatient to get the Ouija board out. She knew that Elizabeth was deeply perplexed—in perfect condition to be staggered by another correct prediction. But she tried to act casual as she headed for her bedroom.

"Liz? Come on," she called out from the stairs of their split-level house.

Elizabeth was standing in the front hallway, taking off her white blazer. She looked up after a pause. "What?"

"Don't you want to find out about your journal?" Jessica asked. She tried to keep the eagerness out of her voice.

Elizabeth seemed to shake herself and then squared her shoulders. "Look, Jess. I know you're convinced about the concert, but I just don't believe the Ouija board is for real," she said slowly, not sounding completely confident.

"We could just try," Jessica pushed. Her instincts told her Elizabeth was weakening. "Come on."

"Well . . ." Elizabeth shrugged and smiled sheepishly. "OK. Just to see what it says."

Jessica grinned. "Great. We don't even need Lila. There'll be just the two of us."

She trotted down the steps and grabbed Elizabeth's hand to drag her up to her room. In less than a minute they were seated on Jessica's bed, setting up the Ouija board that Lila had left behind the night before.

"How do I know you haven't rigged this whole thing?" Elizabeth asked.

"Liz! How can you even think something like that?" Jessica clicked her tongue and pulled down the window shade. She gave her twin an indignant stare.

"Well?" Elizabeth insisted. "Did you?"

Jessica kept her gaze steady. "How many times have you told me never to touch your journal?"

"About a million," Elizabeth replied dryly.

"Well, then." With a slightly injured look on her face, Jessica rested her fingertips on the planchette. She didn't enjoy lying, but if she had to she did.

Elizabeth hesitated for a moment. She sighed and touched the planchette. "OK."

"Good," Jessica breathed. "Now, let's get started. Elizabeth has lost something very important," she intoned. "Can you help her find it?"

Jessica lowered her eyelids and took a deep breath. Then, peeking through her lashes, she began to exert a very slight controlled pressure on the planchette. It was critical to keep it as subtle as possible and to make sure her hands

33

looked relaxed. Hardly breathing, she pushed the marker toward *yes*.

"You're pushing, Jessica," Elizabeth broke in suddenly.

Jessica didn't even blink. Keeping her eyes on Elizabeth, she said, "I am not. Now, do you want to do this or not?"

There was a tense pause until Elizabeth's firm gaze wavered and broke. She nodded faintly. "OK."

"Let's just see what happens," Jessica urged in a gentler tone.

The planchette shifted a bit and then began moving toward the letter *R*. Jessica congratulated herself silently for pulling the planchette toward her without any visible pressure.

"R-E-F-R-I-G— is it refrigerator?" Jessica asked. She stopped all movement.

She and Elizabeth waited. After a whole minute had passed, Jessica shrugged. "I guess that's all we're going to get," she said. "But you wouldn't have put your journal in the refrigerator, would you?"

"No. And besides, someone would've seen it at breakfast," Elizabeth replied, looking doubtful. "That doesn't make any sense."

Jessica bit her lip. "Well, let's look anyway. Come on." She jumped off the bed, then ran

34

down the stairs and to the kitchen. Elizabeth followed more slowly.

"Jessica, it's not in the refrigerator," Elizabeth insisted.

"Let's just think." Jessica put her hands on her hips and faced the refrigerator squarely. "Not in it, maybe . . ."

On tiptoe, Jessica peered over the top of the refrigerator. Elizabeth's journal was at the far edge. "Liz!"

"What? It can't be!" Craning her neck, Elizabeth looked up and reached for her journal. She pulled it down and turned it around in her hands. She frowned in bewilderment. "How did—"

Jessica's eyes lit up. "When you came in from outside, you must have put it up there to get it out of the way, and then you forgot about it," she suggested.

"I guess. . . . That's so strange." Elizabeth looked at her sister. "Jess, do you promise you didn't put it there?"

Jessica nodded solemnly. Once Elizabeth found out it was all a good-natured joke, she would forgive her for lying. "I promise," Jessica vowed.

They stood looking at each other for a tense, expectant moment. Then the sound of a car door slamming broke the silence.

"Mom's home," Jessica said.

Elizabeth looked away. "Right."

As her twin walked slowly out of the kitchen, Jessica allowed herself a grin of satisfaction. It was obviously getting harder for Elizabeth to say she didn't believe in the Ouija board. Just a few more days and she would be completely converted.

She wouldn't lie about a thing like that, would she? Elizabeth asked herself anxiously as she drove to baby-sit at the Bartels.

But if Jessica hadn't put her journal on top of the refrigerator and she hadn't seen Elizabeth put it there, then the Ouija board had actually tracked it down. The way it had known about the concert and her journal couldn't both have been coincidences.

Deep in thought, Elizabeth pulled into the Bartels' driveway. Elsa Bartel was coping with her five-year-old son, Max, by herself, while her husband was away on a long business trip. Max spent his days at a day-care center while Elsa worked, and when she had meetings to attend at night, Elizabeth baby-sat for Max.

"Hi, Liz," Elsa said as she greeted Elizabeth at the front door.

Elizabeth nodded absently. "Hi. How's Max?" she asked, following Elsa into the living room.

"A little cranky. He didn't have a nap to-day," Elsa replied with a warm smile. "He's watching a movie on the VCR right now, but I think he'll be asleep pretty soon."

"Great." With an effort, Elizabeth put the Ouija board out of her mind and focused on her responsibilities. "I'll ask Max if he wants me to read to him," she offered.

Elsa patted her arm. "Terrific. I'll be back by ten."

Elizabeth locked the door behind Elsa, then turned to follow the sound of the TV to find Max. For the rest of the evening, she told herself firmly, she was not going to think about postponed concerts, missing journals, or disturbingly accurate predictions.

At least she would make a real effort not to.

Four

After work on Thursday, Jessica waited in front of the Western Building for Lila to pick her up. Humming to herself, she leaned against the wall and studied faces. She kept up a running commentary with herself on the men that hurried past.

Cute. Definitely cute. His hair is too curly. Now, that one is prime. Hmm. *Too old.*

She flashed a dazzling smile at a young lawyer-type in a three-piece suit strolling by. Then she caught sight of Lila's lime green Triumph pulling up to the curb.

"I won't say what you looked like, scoping all those guys," Lila said, giggling as Jessica clambered in.

Jessica grinned. "I thought I was being subtle."

"Yeah. Subtle as a bulldozer," her friend said with a snort of laughter.

"Go ahead and laugh," Jessica said airily. "But you can't meet good-looking, available men by staring at the sidewalk."

Worn out from working all day, Jessica leaned back and let the late-afternoon sun warm her face as they drove out to the mall.

"Is Lisette's still having a sale?" she asked. Lisette's was one of their favorite stores.

"Yes. And I think I'll get those sandals—you know, the red ones? We'll both go home with lots of new stuff," Lila predicted.

"You more than I." Jessica scrunched up her face into a sour expression as they parked and entered the mall. No matter how hard she tried to save her money, she never had as much as Lila.

Smiling happily, Lila sailed ahead and led the way to the makeup counters, which stretched ahead of them like islands of glitter and sparkling color. Jessica steered her friend to their favorite cosmetics counter, where she examined various lip pencils and lipsticks.

"So, anyway, how'd it go last night?" Lila asked as she tried on some lip gloss. "You know—with Liz?"

Jessica grinned at her friend in the mirror. "Perfect. I stashed her diary on top of the refrigerator, and the Ouija board told her just where to look."

Lila let out a giggle. "That Ouija board is truly amazing!" she drawled sarcastically. "Is she really falling for it?"

"I'm pretty sure she is. And, get this," Jessica added gleefully, her eyes sparkling with mischief. "This afternoon Liz was reading a book in the office. She slammed it shut and put it in her desk when I came over. But . . ."

"But what?" Lila demanded.

Dropping her voice, Jessica said, "I sneaked a look later, and it was called *Beginner's Guide to Occultism*."

"You're kidding!" Hooting with laughter, Lila snatched a tissue and wiped the lip gloss off her mouth. Still giggling, she tried another color. "She's going to be floored when she finds out it's all a big joke."

"You're telling me," Jessica agreed. She cocked her eyebrows. "Let's keep it up until next week, then tell her, OK?"

Lila shook her head. "No way."

"What do you mean?"

"I thought of something else to do—an extension of the original plan," Lila explained. "The ultimate test."

"OK. Shoot."

Moving down the counter, Jessica picked out a peacock-blue eyeliner pencil and began shading under her lashes. She wondered if Lila was getting too zealous about tricking Elizabeth, but she shrugged her doubts away. Jessica fluttered her eyelids rapidly to see how the color looked and waited for Lila to elaborate.

"All right, this is the plan. Say the Ouija board gives Liz some really bad news," Lila began. She hopped up onto a tall stool.

Jessica's gaze slid over to Lila and then back to the mirror. "What kind of bad news?"

"Well, say Liz finds out someone she knows is really sick—"

"Are we talking terminal illness?"

Grinning, Lila nodded her head. "You got it. So what would her reaction be?"

"That's simple," Jessica said. "If it was a friend of hers, she'd be really upset, and she'd be super nice and helpful."

Lila laughed. "Of course she would. But what if it's someone Liz hates— OK, Liz doesn't *hate* anybody," she corrected herself quickly. "But really dislikes. I mean *really* can't stand. Someone we know who gets on her nerves."

There was an expectant pause. Jessica stared at her friend in admiration. She could almost read Lila's mind. "Bruce."

A sneaky smile lit Lila's face. "Exactly."

"Lila, you're brilliant."

Lila bowed from the waist. "Thank you very much."

"But I don't know." Jessica frowned, musing on Lila's latest scheme. "Why would he go along with it?"

"He doesn't even have to know," Lila explained eagerly. She hitched the stool closer and went on in a conspiratorial voice. "The Ouija board will say that Bruce is keeping it a secret."

Jessica snickered, and her eyes glowed. "You've thought of everything."

"Right," Lila agreed with a look of satisfaction. "Liz is going to get all mushy over Bruce, and he won't even know what's going on."

"And she'll think he isn't saying anything about dying because he doesn't want to talk about it, and she won't tell him she knows because she won't want to embarrass him, right?"

Jessica's mind was racing. Lila was right, it was the ultimate test. If Elizabeth could overcome her dislike of Bruce enough to be kind and sympathetic to him, it would definitely prove she believed what the Ouija board said. A laugh of pure delight welled up in Jessica's throat as she imagined her sister's reaction. It would be a priceless scene: Elizabeth in a tug-of-war between her conscience and her disgust for egotistical, infuriating, pain-in-the-neck Bruce Patman.

"This has got to be the juiciest idea you've ever had," Jessica decided finally.

"That's what I think, too."

Lila's eyes twinkled with laughter as she brushed blusher across her cheekbones. When she met Jessica's eyes in the mirror, they both burst into hysterical giggles.

"Girls, is there something I can show you?" a saleswoman asked from behind the counter.

Jessica tried to control herself. "N-no, thank you," she spluttered, keeping a straight face with difficulty.

When the woman drifted away, Jessica and Lila started laughing all over again. Finally Jessica wiped her teary eyes, smearing eyeliner across her temples.

"Let's do it tomorrow night," she gasped, reaching for a tissue.

"But we have to work up to it slowly," warned Lila. "We can't just go, 'Whammo! Bruce is dying.'"

Jessica nodded and let out a weak chuckle. "Right. I'll sneak another look at her journal and find something to use."

"And then . . ."

"And *then*, 'Whammo! Bruce is dying,'" Jessica finished for Lila.

They laughed again, then left the cosmetics counter and continued on with their shopping.

When Lila dropped Jessica off at home, Jessica hesitated a moment before climbing out of the car. "I hope this works," she said doubtfully.

Lila shook her head. "Trust me, Jess. It'll work."

"What if she doesn't believe it, though?"

"She will. She will," Lila insisted.

Jessica shrugged and got out of the car. "I guess we'll know tomorrow night," she concluded, grinning.

"Right. I'll come over around seven-thirty, OK?"

As she slammed the door, Jessica said, "Great. See you tomorrow night."

Lila waved and pulled away from the curb. She was positive her plan would work, but to be sure, she went over it again in her mind.

First Elizabeth would be shocked. Then she would be worried, and then she would start being nice to Bruce. For a long time Lila had suspected that Bruce would have asked Elizabeth out if he'd thought she would say yes— and if it hadn't been for Jeffrey. Lila knew Bruce wasn't likely to ignore an attentive Elizabeth.

If everything worked out as planned, Elizabeth and Bruce would be spending lots of time together before Jeffrey got back from camp. A tender romance would develop, and when Jeffrey returned, Sweet Valley's most rock-solid couple would be on the rocks.

44

And then Jeffrey will be free. For me.

Lila grinned as she drove up the winding road to her house. She had waited a long time for this chance. Ever since Jeffrey first moved to Sweet Valley, Lila had wanted to go out with him. But Elizabeth had gotten in the way. During the school year, Lila had tried several schemes to drive a wedge between Elizabeth and Jeffrey. She had once sabotaged everyone's slam books, saying that Jeffrey was in love with Enid and that Elizabeth was in love with Roger Barrett Patman, Bruce's cousin, who had been legally adopted by the Patmans. For some reason, though, her plots had all backfired. Elizabeth always managed to hang on to Jeffrey.

But not this time, Lila told herself. This time, she was sure her plan was fail-safe.

Lila sighed blissfully as she stopped the car in front of her house. "Lila Fowler, you are a genius," she said aloud.

Five

"This place is dead," Jessica muttered.

Elizabeth gave her twin a quick smile and shook her head. "Poor Jess. Friday is the hardest day to get through, huh?"

"You said it."

Elizabeth pushed her chair back and crossed the newspaper office to the water cooler. A small group of reporters was gathered around the police band radio. They were chatting and drinking water while they waited for interesting news to be broadcast.

"Hi, Liz," Anita Solarz greeted her warmly. Anita was a recently hired staff reporter.

Elizabeth took a cup of water and sipped it. "Anything happening in the world of law and order?"

"Listen for yourself," Anita said. She started counting off on her fingers. "One car accident, no injuries—"

"A woman reported her lawn mower stolen," Seth cut in with a grin.

"Don't forget the barking dog causing a nuisance on Sharon Avenue," added another reporter.

Elizabeth chuckled. "Wow. This sure is a big news day. Which story are you taking?" she asked Seth teasingly.

"I'm not sure. It's a real toss-up." While casual conversation continued around them, Seth leaned over and tuned the radio in more clearly.

"All vehicles in the vicinity of San Rafael Hospital!" The dispatcher's voice cut through the murmur of talk around the water cooler. Instantly everyone snapped to attention. The private hospital was just outside town.

"San Rafael Hospital?" Elizabeth breathed. "The psychiatric—"

"Shh." Seth cut her off.

"Hospital administrator reports patient Donald Redman, Caucasian male, age thirty-two, left the hospital during the night. He is diagnosed as a paranoid schizophrenic, highly excitable, assumed dangerous. Repeat, all vehicles in the vicinity of San Rafael Hospital report to hospital administration building."

47

In seconds everyone within hearing was on the alert, shouting messages across the room and picking up telephones. Elizabeth watched, wide-eyed, as the newsroom came alive and the bulletin was relayed all the way down to Mr. Robb's office. Next to her, Seth clenched his fists in excitement and took her by the arm.

"Come on—we'll be getting assignments as soon as Robb decides."

"This is incredible," she said, hurrying after him. Her heart was pounding. An escaped psychopath was real, hard news. Being in the midst of important news coverage was one of the reasons she had wanted the internship, and she prayed she would have a chance to work on some angle of the story.

A cluster of reporters waited outside Mr. Robb's office, talking loudly and jotting down notes. Every other project in the newsroom seemed to have been abandoned. An expectant hush fell over the group as Mr. Robb's door opened.

"OK. Anita, I want you to go over to San Rafael and interview the staff on Redman's behavior," Mr. Robb announced crisply. He jabbed the air with his finger as he pointed. "Pete, you keep track of the police investigation, and, Seth, I want Redman's case history. My source says he's a Sweet Valley native. Got it? OK, get to work, everyone."

The crowd scattered, buzzing with excitement. Elizabeth followed Seth to his desk, just stopping to snatch a pencil and a notepad from her own desk as she passed it.

"What should I do?" she asked.

Seth ran one hand through his hair and frowned. "OK, first, if this guy is from Sweet Valley, let's see if he went to school here. Then we need to find out where he lived and what he did to end up in the nuthouse."

"I can get in touch with the high school principal," Elizabeth said, rapidly scribbling on her pad. "I know him pretty well, and I'll try to reach some of the secretaries, too."

"Good. If I try to get his medical records, I know I'll be stonewalled, but we'll find something. Check with me in an hour, and we'll see what we've got."

Elizabeth nodded and hurried back to her desk. The excitement in the air was tangible, and she paused for a moment to relish the thrill of being in the middle of a serious, fast-breaking news story. She bit back a smile of pure elation and pulled the telephone toward her.

"You look like you're about to have a fit,"

Jessica said. She leaned against Elizabeth's desk, her arms folded, a lopsided smile on her face.

"Well, come on!" Elizabeth looked up at her twin in surprise. "Don't you think this is pretty exciting?"

Jessica shrugged and fiddled with one of her earrings. "Not really. The police will get him before the paper even gets to press."

"Pessimist," Elizabeth muttered as she leafed through the phone book.

"*I'm* a pessimist because I think the police will find an escaped lunatic before he starts parading through Sweet Valley with a chain saw?"

"You know what I mean."

"Yeah, well . . ." Jessica grinned and pushed away from the desk. "You're just wasting your time."

Elizabeth sent Jessica a pointed look and turned her back on her.

Forty-five minutes later Elizabeth pulled a chair up to Seth's desk and flipped through her notepad. "OK, this is what I've got," she announced. "Redman was a straight-A student at Sweet Valley High, in the science club, with a special interest in electronics," Elizabeth read. "But he was suspended several times for disruptive behavior. He started fights with teachers when they disagreed with him." She frowned.

50

"Also, his record says in his senior year he was fixated on this one girl, sort of obsessed with her, I guess. He kept following her around and annoying her."

Seth was listening intently, and his eyes kindled with satisfaction. "Great. It fits with what I've got. Some guys never give up," he added in a cynical tone.

"No kidding," Elizabeth agreed wryly. "The secretary I spoke to was there when he was a student. She says the girl was homecoming queen, dated the football team captain—very popular. But Redman was a real pest. He kept asking her out and thought everyone else was trying to come between them when she kept saying no."

Seth frowned. "I guess that's part of the paranoia thing—being really aggressive and thinking people are trying to sabotage you. It fits with his attitude toward the teachers, too. I'll get a quote from a shrink on that," he added to himself. He scrawled something on a piece of paper. "What else do you have?"

Elizabeth scanned her notes. "Well, there's something in his school record they wouldn't tell me about, and then the last thing is that he was expelled. Maybe something to do with the girl?" she ventured.

"Could be." Seth took a deep breath and

tapped a pencil against his palm. "In his senior year he started getting arrested—disturbing the peace, threatening people, neighbors complaining, that sort of thing."

Elizabeth shook her head. "That probably includes Miss Homecoming," she mused. She glanced up at Seth, who had fallen silent. He was watching her expectantly. "What?" she prompted.

"You're right," he said, examining his notes. "His police record also includes kidnapping."

Stunned, Elizabeth gaped at him. "What? The girl?" she added with a flash of insight. "That could be why he was expelled."

Seth leaned back and crossed his arms. "Yep. It was only for one day, but he was definitely holding her against her will."

"Is that why he was committed?"

"Ah!" Seth grinned triumphantly and folded his hands behind his neck. "That's the exciting part," he said in a mysterious voice.

Elizabeth punched his knee, and gave him an ominous scowl. "Come on. What was it?"

The reporter cleared his throat for effect. "Seems that a couple of years after he abducted the girl and got kicked out of school, our Mr. Redman tried to kill his father and mother—with a bomb."

"What?"

"Yeah. He's some sort of electronics genius, like you said. He made a bomb the police almost couldn't handle. Apparently it was highly sophisticated, even for a professional."

Elizabeth let her breath out slowly. "But why?" she gasped, horrified. "Why would he try to kill his own parents?"

"Who knows?" Seth tipped his head to one side. "The paranoid personality is very touchy. Any kind of grudge this guy had could have been blown way out of proportion. Maybe his father and mother did something he didn't approve of—like making him get psychiatric treatment."

"I wouldn't blame them if they did," Elizabeth muttered. "If he was so out of control . . ."

Seth nodded grimly. "Right. And maybe he didn't particularly want to. Let's see if we can narrow it down a bit more. This is a good start, but we need a lot more material. We've just scratched the surface. We need to know where he lived, who his neighbors were, what his home life was like, where his family is now—"

"Wait, wait," Elizabeth begged, scribbling frantically. She paused and looked up at Seth. "Thanks for letting me help."

Seth cleared his throat gruffly. "Yeah, well, get to work, OK? We've got a deadline."

Hiding a smile, Elizabeth stood up and nodded. "Sure thing."

"Oh, and he had a sister. See if you can find out anything about her," Seth added in a brisk, businesslike tone.

Elizabeth made a note. "Got it."

Within minutes she was deeply absorbed in her research on Redman's school history again. The deeper she dug, the more Seth's observation about paranoia haunted her. Any grudge Redman had could be blown completely out of proportion. Would the escaped man return to Sweet Valley to settle an old score?

Biting her lip, Elizabeth lowered her pencil and stared off into space. If that was Redman's plan, she hoped Jessica was right about the police catching him. The sooner Redman was found and taken back to San Rafael, the safer Sweet Valley would be.

By the time she was ready to leave the newspaper office, all Elizabeth could think about was Donald Redman. Seth's preliminary article on Redman's past was ready for press. There were still many gaps, and so far, the police hadn't found any trace of the man. He was simply too wily to leave a trail. Elizabeth was beginning to

54

wonder if they were only seeing the tip of the iceberg on the Donald Redman story.

"Steve's picking you up, right?" she asked Jessica as she straightened up her desk.

Her twin nodded. "Yep. How late are you baby-sitting?"

"Till eight or nine," Elizabeth answered. Something in her sister's tone caught her ear. "Why?"

"It's just that Lila's coming over, and we're going to ask the Ouija board some more questions, that's all." Writing busily on a legal pad, Jessica kept her head down.

Elizabeth paused. The news about Redman had been so engrossing that she hadn't thought about the Ouija board all day. Now all the strange, confusing questions about it came flooding back. She avoided meeting Jessica's eyes as she said casually, "Maybe I'll do it with you guys when I get back."

"Sure. If you want to."

A guilty blush colored Elizabeth's cheeks as she hurried away. Despite telling herself that the Ouija board was all hype, on a gut level she couldn't resist wanting to find out more. She felt a little ashamed of herself, though, since, as a reporter, she was supposed to confine herself to facts.

Her mind racing, Elizabeth drove out of the parking garage and headed for Mrs. Bartel's house. A whirl of thoughts and images spun through her head: Redman, bombs, occult messages, inexplicable coincidences, and crazy paranoias.

"I'll go crazy myself if I don't think about something else," she finally said aloud, shaking her head. She laughed at herself as she climbed out of the car and headed for the Bartels' front door.

"Hi, Liz," Elsa said, greeting her at the door. "Come on in."

Elizabeth smiled as she followed Mrs. Bartel into the cozy house. "How's everything today?"

"Fine. Just fine. And here's a good boy!" Elsa laughed as five-year-old Max ran into her arms. She hoisted him up onto her hip, and Max turned wide brown eyes on Elizabeth.

"Hi, Max," Elizabeth said with a grin.

He ducked his head into his mother's shoulder.

"Oh, don't be so silly." Elsa chuckled. She shook her head and grinned knowingly at Elizabeth. "He's been excited all day because he knew you were coming."

"He's a doll," Elizabeth said. She winked at Max as he sneaked a look at her, and then she laughed when he hid his face again.

Elsa carried him into the kitchen. "His dinner's all ready, and there's cold chicken and salad for you. I'll be at this meeting until eight or so." Elsa Bartel was on the board of directors of the day-care center Max attended, and organizing new projects took a lot of her time.

"That's fine."

"So, what are tomorrow's headlines?" Elsa asked in a cheerful tone.

Elizabeth had been trying to tease shy Max into saying hello, but Elsa's question jolted her.

"Pretty exciting stuff," she said, her eyes glowing with excitement. "A man named Donald Redman escaped from the psychiatric hospital in San Rafael today. No one knows where he is, but he may be hiding out in Sweet Valley, and he may be dangerous. Come on, Max," she coaxed, looking at the little boy again. They played peekaboo until Elsa's silence finally caught her attention. When Elizabeth looked up, Mrs. Bartel's face was chalky white.

"He's coming—here?" Elsa whispered.

You jerk, Elizabeth scolded herself. In her enthusiasm about the news, she hadn't thought about the effect it would have on a young mother alone in a house with a little child. Of course Elsa would be frightened. A dangerous psychotic prowling around town would make anyone nervous.

"I'm—I'm sure the police will find him really soon," Elizabeth went on hastily. "They're putting his picture in the paper, and the whole police force is on the case," she said reassuringly.

Still pale, Elsa let Max slip gently down to the floor. She twisted her fingers together and sent an apprehensive glance toward the front hall.

"We'll be just fine." Elizabeth tried to sound cheerful and unconcerned, but inwardly she was kicking herself for being so tactless and insensitive.

Elsa managed a faint smile. "Well . . . I don't *really* have to go to this meeting," she said. Her hands clenched and unclenched periodically. "It's not so important, and I think I'd feel better if—"

"I understand," Elizabeth assured her. "Would you like me to stay anyway and keep you company?"

"Oh, that's sweet of you." Mrs. Bartel smiled and shook her head. "But I'll be fine. I didn't really want to go to this meeting, anyway. You just go and enjoy your Friday night."

"Well, OK. I'm sorry I gave you such a shock, though."

"Don't worry about it," Elsa insisted. She led Elizabeth toward the front door. "I'm glad you told me. Really. And I'm sure they'll catch him before too long. Could you come Monday evening for a couple of hours? The board is taking a vote, so I can't miss that meeting."

"Sure. I'll see you on Monday." Elizabeth stepped outside. "Bye."

As Elizabeth headed home, she berated herself for spilling the story in such a cold-hearted way. She could still see the stunned look on Elsa's face.

But Elizabeth was happy to have the whole evening unexpectedly free. Jessica and Lila were sure to be waiting for her at home—with the Ouija board.

Six

"Hi." Jessica, in her bathing suit, greeted Lila at the front door. "Let's go out back. I want to swim a few laps, if you don't mind."

"Sure." Lila followed Jessica through the hall to the kitchen, where they stopped to grab two diet sodas from the refrigerator.

"We have to get this story down cold," Lila began in an authoritative tone.

Jessica nodded as she snapped open her can. "I know. Come on."

She opened the sliding glass door in the dining room that led to the patio. After setting her soda down on the arm of a lounge chair, Jessica dove into the pool and concentrated on swimming laps. There was plenty of time to work out their story before Elizabeth came home, she figured. And besides, if she wanted to keep her cheerleader's figure, she had to spend time doing more than just sitting at an office desk.

At last she pulled herself out and wrapped a huge towel around her, sarong-style. Then she lay down in the chair next to Lila and reached for her soda. "OK. Shoot."

"Sure you don't want to go running or something, first?" Lila drawled. "Maybe a couple of sets of tennis?"

Jessica sent her friend a withering look. "Very funny. Come on, let's get this worked out so we do it perfectly."

"Fine. Just checking." Lila became businesslike and serious as she continued. "First, I think we should make the Ouija board seem like it doesn't want to cooperate."

"Like it doesn't want us to know, right?"

Lila nodded and took a sip of her diet soda. "Right. But then I'll demand to know the truth. If it's important, we have a right to know, I'll say." Lila curled her legs up under her and frowned. "What should Bruce have?" she added.

Jessica snickered. "How about the plague?"

"Can you die of leprosy?" Lila asked with a malicious giggle. "I mean, if he's got to go, he might as well have something really interesting."

"A disfiguring disease," Jessica spluttered. "First he loses all his hair—"

Lila cut her off with a shriek of laughter. "Then his teeth fall out!"

"Poor Bruce," Jessica purred. "What a way to go."

They both grinned mischievously. The smiles disappeared from their faces, however, when they heard a car's engine.

"Isn't that the Fiat?" Lila whispered, wide-eyed with alarm.

Jessica nodded tersely. "Liz is home early. Just be cool."

When Elizabeth came out onto the patio a few moments later, Jessica and Lila were calmly discussing whether to see a movie or go to the Beach Disco.

"Hi, guys."

Jessica looked up and pretended to be surprised. "Liz! I thought you weren't coming home till a lot later."

"Mrs. Bartel decided not to go out when I told her about that escaped psychopath," Elizabeth explained.

Lila shivered. "That gives me the creeps."

"I wonder what would happen if we asked the Ouija board where Redman is?" Jessica suggested.

Elizabeth and Lila both looked at her doubtfully, and Jessica raised her voice. "Just a thought."

"Well . . ." Elizabeth kicked her shoes off and stepped onto the top step of the pool. The water lapped around her ankles, and Jessica and Lila watched her silently. "Why not?"

Jessica did not dare to glance at Lila for fear of Elizabeth noticing. But inwardly she smiled. Sensible, no-nonsense Elizabeth was hooked.

Shrugging, Lila said, "Sure. Why not?"

"OK. Then let's do it." Jessica wrapped her towel around her more tightly and led the way up to her room. Once the shades were drawn and the lights dimmed, they were ready. This time Jessica and Lila rested their fingertips on the planchette.

Lila wet her lips. "We are frightened. We may all be in danger," she said in a hushed voice. "There is a man who could hurt us if he isn't found."

The planchette was motionless. Sitting beside Jessica on the floor, Elizabeth shifted uneasily.

"Can't you help us?" Lila continued. "It could be a matter of life and death."

Under their fingers, the planchette suddenly jerked. It traveled to the word *yes*.

"What does that mean?" Elizabeth whispered.

"Yes, it can help, or yes, it's a matter of life and death?"

Lila shrugged. "I don't know. We have to keep asking. Is someone in danger?" she asked in her solemn voice.

The planchette moved to the word *yes* again.

"From Redman?"

The pointer moved to *no*.

The three girls looked at one another in surprise. "I don't get it," Jessica muttered. "Lila, you keep asking."

"Right. Umm." Lila considered for a moment and then nodded. "Who is in danger?"

There was a brief hesitation, and then the planchette moved to the alphabet. "B-P," it spelled.

Jessica drew her breath in sharply. "That must be the initials." She looked at her sister's concentrated expression. "It could be anyone. It doesn't even have to be someone we know."

"Well, keep asking," Elizabeth said in a somewhat worried tone.

Lila sniffed. "Right. Is BP going to have an accident? Bad luck?"

"I-L-L. S-E-C-R-E-T," the board spelled.

Lila jerked her hands away from the planchette. "I don't like this," she said, shaking her head. "This is too creepy."

"Lila, please." Elizabeth's voice was pleading. "It could be important."

Across the board, Jessica and Lila shared a secret, triumphant look. So far, it was going perfectly. Lila was playing her role like a pro, and Elizabeth was completely enthralled.

"Well . . ." Lila sounded reluctant. Then she sighed. "I guess we should figure it out. Is BP someone we know?"

Slowly the planchette inched toward *yes*.

"Oh, no," Jessica moaned. She swallowed hard, relishing the drama. "Someone we know is sick, sick enough to be in danger. BP. BP. It's—"

Elizabeth cut in. "Bruce? Bruce *Patman*?" She looked at her twin, her eyes wide and anxious. "Do you think it could really be Bruce?"

Jessica shrugged silently.

"I'll find out," Lila offered. "Is it Bruce Patman?"

The planchette moved to *yes*.

"He's very sick? Is he—is he dying?"

The planchette quivered, but stayed on *yes*.

Elizabeth gasped. "Oh, no."

"What does 'secret' mean?" Lila continued, her voice low and intense. "Doesn't he know?"

"K-N-O-W-S" was the answer.

"*He* knows, but no one else does," Elizabeth

65

whispered with conviction. "That must be what it means."

"Is it that he doesn't want anyone to know he's dying?" Lila asked.

Yes.

Jessica closed her eyes briefly. "I can't believe this. I just can't. Bruce is so—" She left her sentence unfinished.

"He has been looking sort of—I don't know, tired, maybe," Lila said hesitantly. "But I'm probably imagining it."

"No." Elizabeth shook her head. "No, I've noticed it, too. But I never thought . . ."

Shaking her head, Lila put her fingertips on the planchette again. "Is there anything else you can tell us about Bruce?"

They waited in hushed silence for a minute, but there was no response.

"I guess that's it," Jessica said in a tone of regret. Privately she was glad Lila had decided to quit. Pushing the planchette without being obvious about it took a lot of muscle control and concentration.

Elizabeth was silent, brooding. Finally she seemed to wake up. "You know, I've never really liked Bruce," she confessed. "But if this is true, we can't just ignore it. Maybe he acts the way he does because he's scared of dying. Maybe—" She shook her head.

"I know one way to find out of it's true," Lila spoke up. "We can ask him."

"No!" Elizabeth shook her head vehemently. "He doesn't want anyone to know! Don't you see? He's been putting up a front all this time. It might be the only way he has of dealing with what he's going through." She bit her lower lip. "I think we should respect that."

Jessica looked doubtful. "Yeah, but—"

"Don't ask him," Elizabeth insisted. "I guess he wants to save his pride."

"Well, I know one thing," said Lila, looking glum. "Even if we don't ask him, I know I'll act differently around him. I mean, I guess I feel sorry for the guy."

"Me, too," Jessica agreed solemnly.

Elizabeth nodded. "Yeah. It's so awful. I almost wish we didn't know. But I'm glad," she corrected herself. "At least we can go easier on him now."

"Hey." Lila brightened. "I think I heard him tell someone he was going to the Beach Disco tonight. Let's all go."

"Good idea," Jessica chimed in. Trust Lila to have phase two all ready to put into operation. "We were thinking about going anyway. Come on, Liz. How about it?"

Elizabeth hesitated. She wondered if she

should go without Jeffrey, but then she squared her shoulders. "Sure. Why not?"

Jessica jumped up. "Great! Lila, you can borrow something of mine so we don't have to go to your house first. Let's try to get there by eight."

Shortly after eight o'clock Elizabeth, Jessica, and Lila arrived at the sprawling redwood building perched above the beach. Lights on the deck shone on the sand, and music drifted out to the parking lot. The girls slammed the car doors and headed for the disco.

"Looks crowded tonight," Jessica observed happily, taking a look at the number of cars in the parking lot.

Elizabeth nodded. Her eyes were drawn to the black Porsche parked near the entrance. *Bruce is here*, she told herself. *Poor guy. I just can't believe it.*

Deep in thought, she followed her sister and Lila inside. On the threshold she stopped to let her eyes adjust to the flashing lights. By the time she recovered, Jessica and Lila had melted into the crowd.

Elizabeth felt a bit strange being there without Jeffrey, but she didn't let it bother her. She was just there to relax, she thought, and possibly to say a few kinds words to Bruce. Thinking over all the cutting remarks she had made to him in the past made her feel sick with guilt. At least she had a chance to make it up to him.

As Elizabeth skirted around the throng of dancers, she kept looking for Bruce. She felt as though she *had* to speak to him, to let him know he had her support in his time of crisis. People kept bumping into her and blocking her view. Then, suddenly, she saw Bruce leaning against the wall just ahead of her.

"Bruce! Hi," she called, giving him a warm smile.

Bruce turned and saw her, and his dark eyebrows rose a fraction in surprise. "Hey, Goldilocks."

"So." Elizabeth didn't know what to say. Suddenly shy, she looked away. "What's new?"

Bruce looked even more surprised, but he smiled crookedly. "Not much—Liz . . ." There was a hint of question in his voice.

She laughed. "Yes, I'm Liz," she assured him.

"What are you doing here without Jeffrey?" He folded his arms across his chest and cocked his head to one side.

Elizabeth smiled. "I can function without him, you know. I guess I just came to see—" She stopped herself before saying "you."

It was strange, she thought. Before tonight,

she would have thought Bruce was being his usual arrogant self. But now she could tell it was all a bluff.

A silence fell between them. Bruce looked at her appraisingly, as though trying to figure out what she was thinking. Then, as the music changed to a slow tune, he said, "You want to dance?"

Without hesitating, Elizabeth nodded. She knew Bruce was a good dancer, and there was no telling how much longer he would be able to enjoy himself. Elizabeth willingly let him take her hand and lead her out onto the dance floor.

"How are you, anyway?" she couldn't resist asking as she looked up into his handsome face.

"Just fine," Bruce murmured, grinning at her. "Just fine."

Elizabeth's heart welled with emotion. Bruce was being so brave by pretending there was nothing wrong, she realized. For a moment she thought she might cry.

"So, what was it I said, anyway?" Bruce asked after they had been dancing for a while.

"What?" Elizabeth looked at him, puzzled.

He gave her another crooked smile. "You don't usually have much to say to me. So I was wondering what changed your mind."

"I just . . ."

Raising her eyes to his, Elizabeth gave Bruce a long, meaningful look, trying to communicate her sympathy and support without bringing the subject out in the open. If he wanted to deal with it alone, she would respect that wish. "Nothing," she said in a choked voice.

Bruce returned her look evenly. "OK by me," he replied, his voice smooth and caressing. He tightened his arms around her.

Poor Bruce, Elizabeth thought. *You don't have to pretend.* She rested her cheek against his shoulder and sighed. *Poor Bruce.*

Seven

The beach was as crowded as always on Saturday afternoon. Elizabeth and Enid had gotten there early, but by three o'clock they were surrounded on all sides. Elizabeth laid on her stomach with her chin propped up on her fists and stared moodily out at the Pacific. She knew she was ignoring her friend, but she couldn't help being preoccupied.

"You seem depressed," Enid said quietly. "Are you all right?"

Elizabeth smiled and shook her head. "I'm fine."

"If you want to talk about it, whatever it is . . ."

"I know. Thanks."

Absently Elizabeth scooped up a handful of sand and let it trickle through her fingers. She wished she could talk to Enid about what was troubling her, but she couldn't. At first she had not wanted to admit how interested she had become in the Ouija board predictions, and now . . .

She sighed, thinking back to the night before. Bruce had outdone himself to be charming. In fact, he had been almost sweet. It was hard to believe he was terminally ill. After all, nothing about his actions or his words proved anything one way or the other. It was all inconclusive. Elizabeth was almost tempted not to believe the Ouija board, but then she remembered all the accurate predictions it had made. Bruce was dying, and she couldn't talk to anyone about it. Not Enid, not Jeffrey, not even Bruce himself.

"Tonight was supposed to be the Endless Summer concert," Elizabeth said, thinking out loud.

"I know. I'm still angry about them postponing it."

Privately Elizabeth agreed with Enid. More than anything, she wished the concert were going on as originally planned. That would mean the Ouija board was wrong and she wouldn't have to accept what it predicted.

Beside her, Enid sat up and rummaged through her beach bag for a book.

"Oh, great," Enid muttered. "Here comes Bruce Patman and his electric ego. He's headed right this way, too."

A warm blush colored Elizabeth's cheeks. "Hey, go easy on him, all right?"

Enid regarded Elizabeth with surprise.

"Hi, Liz. Hi, Enid." Bruce stopped in front of them, his shadow falling across their blanket. In white tennis shorts and a royal-blue shirt, he looked handsome and full of self-confidence. "How's the water today?"

"Same as always," Enid replied skeptically.

Elizabeth smiled and sat up. "Hi, Bruce. Why don't you sit down?"

"I thought you'd never ask."

As Bruce stretched out next to Elizabeth, Enid gave them both a puzzled, slightly frosty look. "I think I'll go swimming," she announced.

Elizabeth almost stopped her friend. Obviously it seemed peculiar for her to be so friendly to Bruce, especially with Jeffrey away. But she couldn't explain that it was all perfectly innocent. "See you later," Elizabeth said, looking down at her feet. Enid walked away, and for a few minutes neither Elizabeth nor Bruce spoke.

"I had a good time last night," Bruce said eventually. "You really know how to make life worth living," he added in a light, humorous tone.

Elizabeth's heart gave a lurch. She looked at him searchingly, hardly breathing. Bruce leaned back on one elbow and gazed at her, a devilish smile lighting up his dark eyes.

"What do you mean?" Elizabeth said at last. Bruce had come close to mentioning the awful truth, and if encouraged, Elizabeth hoped he would open up to her.

Bruce shrugged. "Just that I'm really glad you came last night."

"Oh."

Elizabeth nodded and looked away, digging her toes into the hot sand. Apparently Bruce couldn't bring himself to discuss his illness yet, but he had come very close. Keeping up his usual ironic tone of voice was just his self-defense mechanism, she realized now.

"Do you feel like walking?" Bruce asked.

"Are you sure you feel up to it?" Elizabeth said anxiously.

Bruce grinned. "With you, sure."

That was all the answer Elizabeth needed. If she was helping to cheer him up and take his mind off his pain and trouble, she would gladly keep him company. Smiling tenderly, Elizabeth hopped to her feet. "Which way?"

Bruce gestured toward the left. As they started walking he draped one arm across Elizabeth's shoulders. He looked down at her, his eyes sparkling. "You know, you're OK, Goldilocks."

Elizabeth laughed. She could see right through his macho attitude. "You're not so bad, either."

They walked that way for a few steps, and then Elizabeth edged out from under his arm. She didn't want anyone to get the wrong impression. What she felt for Bruce was a warm, compassionate friendship, but she could see how walking so close might be misunderstood.

He looked at her with a question in his eyes, and Elizabeth gave him a warm, encouraging smile.

"Did you see that?" Jessica twisted around on their blanket and stared at Lila in shock.

Lila opened one eye sleepily. "Huh?"

"Bruce just had his arm around my sister!" Jessica turned and stared down the beach again, where Elizabeth and Bruce were walking together along the shoreline. They seemed to be deep in conversation.

"No kidding?" Lila sat up, grinning. "I guess she's trying to help ease the burden."

"Yeah, well, believe me, Bruce is feeling no pain," Jessica retorted.

Lila let out a short laugh and tilted her face back to the sun.

Frowning, Jessica hugged her knees to her chin and looked at the water. A joke was a joke, but still, she didn't want Bruce Patman getting the wrong idea about Elizabeth. It was beginning to appear as though the plan was working *too* well.

"I don't think it's so funny anymore," she grumbled.

Lila straightened up and started to rub suntan lotion on her arms. She looked pensive. "I don't know. I think they make a cute couple."

"They're *not* a couple, Li. Not Liz and that— that egotistical jerk." Jessica sneered.

"I seem to remember you went out with that 'jerk' yourself," Lila said, giving Jessica a sidelong glance. "He can't be that bad."

"Yeah, well, he is, and you know it," Jessica snapped. She hated to be reminded of her own brief infatuation with Bruce. "He doesn't exactly play fair, you know. He'll do anything to get what he wants."

Lila pretended to be shocked. "But Liz is going out with Jeffrey."

"And that's the way it's going to stay."

In the past, Jessica had often poked her nose into Elizabeth's relationships, trying to stir up trouble. But for Lila to do it struck her as unfair. After all, Elizabeth wasn't Lila's twin sister.

Jessica pouted and glared at Lila as a new thought occurred to her. "Did you call Bruce when you went to get those sodas before?'' she demanded.

"Me? Call Bruce Patman? On the *telephone*?'' Lila's voice kept rising higher and higher in indignation, but her eyes were dancing with laughter.

"Right, Lila. You're as pure as snow,'' Jessica said scathingly. "Now, come on. Let's tell her today.''

"Tell her what?''

"Tell her it's all a joke,'' Jessica said. "It's gone on long enough.''

For a few seconds Lila concentrated on massaging lotion on her legs. Her face was a mask. Then, in a low voice, she said, "If you tell her it was a joke, you'll have to tell her you read her *personal* letters.''

Jessica opened her mouth to speak, then snapped it shut.

"You read her journal,'' Lila went on smoothly. "You deliberately lied about hiding it, and you did everything but take a lie detector test to prove the Ouija board was for real.''

Jessica squirmed. Her snooping, spying, and lying were serious enough to make Elizabeth distrust her for the rest of their lives. Suddenly she didn't know how she had let Lila talk her into doing anything so devious.

"Yeah, but—''

Lila lifted her eyebrows. "But what?"

Fuming, Jessica flopped down on her stomach and buried her face in her arms. There had to be a way to wriggle out of this mess.

"You know, I was thinking," Lila purred. "I thought up something else for the Ouija board to tell Liz."

Jessica groaned. "Lila!"

"Well? Are you in or out?"

Jessica was backed into a corner, and she knew it. "In," she said, her voice muffled.

"What?"

Jessica sat up and whirled around on her friend. "In! I said in, OK?"

Lila smiled. "That's what I thought you said."

When Lila arrived at the Wakefields' for dinner, she was just in time to see Bruce's black Porsche disappearing around the corner. Her mouth curved into a sly, catlike smile as she pulled into the driveway.

So far, so good, she told herself happily. *In a couple more days, Liz and Bruce will be crazy about each other.*

"Did I just see Bruce leaving?" she asked as she joined Jessica and Elizabeth in the kitchen.

Jessica, who was making a salad, sent her friend an irritated look, but Elizabeth smiled.

"He drove me home from the beach. You know, he's really not as conceited and egotistical as we always thought," Elizabeth said thoughtfully. She sat down at the table.

Looking interested, Lila pulled out a chair and sat across from Elizabeth. "Really? How is he, though? I mean, do you think he's really dying?"

Elizabeth toyed with the salt shaker. "Well, he hasn't said anything about it, but sometimes he'll say something ambiguous. It's almost as if he wants to talk about it but won't."

Lila kept a perfectly straight face, but inside, she was shaking with laughter.

And you said Jess and I were gullible, she crowed silently. *You win the prize, Liz.*

"Hi, girls." Mrs. Wakefield walked into the kitchen and took some chicken breasts out of the refrigerator to start dinner. "Hi, Lila."

"Hi, Mrs. Wakefield."

"Liz, was that Bruce Patman who dropped you off? I didn't know you were friends."

Elizabeth looked uncomfortable. "Well, you see—"

"We all have to go upstairs now, Mom," Jessica interrupted. "No one's supposed to know, remember?" she hissed at Elizabeth as they hurried out of the kitchen.

Lila stifled a giggle and ran up the stairs of

80

the split-level house after the twins. Once safely in Jessica's room, they closed the door. Lila picked the planchette up off Jessica's bureau and turned it over and over in her hands.

"I wish we'd never started this whole thing," she said softly, watching Elizabeth from under her lashes. "Some things are better left unknown."

Just as she guessed, Elizabeth disagreed. "Not necessarily, Lila."

"Listen, I don't want to do it anymore," Jessica said in a loud voice. She gave Lila a severe look, but it was ignored.

"Just once more, OK?" Elizabeth suggested.

"Well—OK. If Jessica wants to." Lila turned wide, innocent eyes on Jessica. "Jess?"

Scowling, Jessica looked from Lila to Elizabeth and back again. She folded her arms and made a face. "All right," she said through clenched teeth.

"Good." Elizabeth sighed with relief, sat down on the floor, and opened up the Ouija board.

"Is there a message for anyone here?" Lila asked when they were ready. This time Lila and Elizabeth had their fingertips on the planchette. "Does anyone want to communicate with one of us?"

Lila flashed Jessica a warning glance. She didn't want Jessica to back down and ruin the plan at this stage of the game. She pushed the planchette gently toward the letter *E*.

"That's me," Elizabeth whispered, her eyes fixed on the board.

"Right," Lila agreed. "Who wants to speak to Elizabeth?" She kept her hands motionless. Jessica gave her a puzzled frown. But Lila made no response.

Elizabeth wet her lips nervously. "What does that mean?"

"I don't know," Lila said. "I'll ask again. Who wants to communicate with Elizabeth?"

When there was still no answer, Elizabeth sighed. "It's not working."

"You're right," Lila agreed, nodding thoughtfully. She was especially proud of herself for that touch: If the Ouija board only worked occasionally, it seemed more temperamental and less like she or Jessica was controlling it. And evidently Elizabeth was now a wholehearted believer, thanks to Lila's crafty manipulating.

"Oh, well," Lila sighed. She shrugged regretfully. "I guess we'll never know."

"Do you think it could be Bruce?" Elizabeth hazarded. She frowned. "Or Jeffrey? Or—" She shook her head, perplexed.

Lila was thrilled that Elizabeth thought of Bruce before Jeffrey. Her plan was working out just the way she wanted it to.

"It could be nothing at all," Jessica pointed out sourly. She gave Lila a disgusted look. "Anyway, I'm not spending my whole Saturday night asking stupid questions. I'm going to see if dinner's ready."

"OK," Lila said. She looked at Elizabeth. "Maybe tomorrow we can find out who's trying to reach you."

Elizabeth nodded, deep in thought. "Maybe," she agreed absently. "Maybe."

Eight

"This has got to be the most boring job in the whole world," Jessica complained, biting into her sandwich. Her mouth full, she mumbled, "There's *nothing* happening around here."

Elizabeth turned the newspaper page without commenting. Usually Mondays were busy at the *Sweet Valley News*, but for some reason things had been slow that morning. At the moment the office was quiet because most of the staff was out to lunch. Elizabeth reached for her soda while she scanned the second-page articles.

"And that whole psycho killer story was a big flop, too," Jessica went on. She elbowed some books out of the way so she would have more room. "Some major news flash *that* was."

"He didn't actually kill anyone," Elizabeth corrected automatically. She turned back to the front page and frowned at the lead story again.

So far, the police hadn't turned up any more information on Donald Redman, and he hadn't made any threats or tried to harm anyone. The man seemed to have vanished without a trace. Maybe he had run as far away from his hometown as possible. Maybe he didn't have a vendetta against his old "enemies" the way everyone had expected.

But privately, Elizabeth thought he might. Anita Solarz had done some deeper research on Redman's kidnapping episode and discovered interesting facts. The girl Redman had fallen for had been pretty but insensitive. Instead of letting Redman down easily, she had teased and taunted him. Her popular and exclusive clique—football players and their girlfriends—had waged a campaign of practical jokes and insults against him. According to Anita, they turned Redman and his unrequited love into the joke of Sweet Valley High. Evidently that was one of the things that had sent him over the edge and driven him to kidnap the girl. Judging by everything else she had learned about Redman, Elizabeth suspected he might still be steaming over it.

Jessica craned her neck to look at Redman's photograph. "If I saw that guy, I'd have a heart attack on the spot. He looks so bizarre."

Elizabeth couldn't help laughing. She looked

at her twin in amusement. "Jess, if you met this guy without knowing who he was, you'd probably want to go out with him."

"Ugh. No way." Jessica managed a dramatic shiver and dropped her sandwich in disgust.

Elizabeth shook her head and studied the picture. Redman looked like a completely normal and attractive man. There was nothing at all in his appearance to show that he was dangerously off-balance.

"Hey, Liz?"

The innocent tone in her sister's voice immediately caught Elizabeth's attention. She glanced up and raised one eyebrow. "Yesss?" she drawled.

Jessica looked hurt. "What?"

"You want something, I can tell," Elizabeth said. "You had that Liz-you're-the-sweetest-person-in-the-world-can-you-do-me-a-favor look in your eyes."

"Well . . ." Jessica toyed with a pencil, her eyes downcast. Then the dimple in her left cheek popped into view, and she sneaked a look at Elizabeth from under her lashes. "Actually, I was hoping . . ."

Elizabeth heaved a sigh. Jessica was always trying to wheedle out of something—or *into* something. Elizabeth sat back and crossed her arms. "OK, what is it this time?"

"I was just thinking, since it's so dead here

today— See, Lila asked if I wanted to catch the two o'clock matinee at the Valley Cinema, and I thought maybe you could just tell people I'm at the public library doing research for an article on the wine grape harvest," Jessica explained in a rush.

Elizabeth nodded thoughtfully and pursed her lips. "What's playing?" she said.

"Terror in the Subway, Part Four." Jessica brightened visibly. "So? What do you say?"

Elizabeth slumped down in her chair and squeezed her eyes shut. "You want me to cover up for you so you can go see something that incredibly stupid?"

"Right."

"Well . . ."

Jessica hunched forward. "You don't even have to say anything if you don't want to. But if anyone asks, just say I was *talking* about doing research for the grape harvest article." Jessica sat back and grinned triumphantly. "And since I just this moment talked about it, you'd be telling the truth."

"Jessica." Elizabeth balled up her lunch bag and tossed it from one hand to the other. "I don't know why I let you get away with this kind of thing all the time."

"I knew you'd say yes!" Jessica crowed. She jumped out of her seat and hugged Elizabeth.

"Because you are the sweetest, nicest sister in the world."

"Yeah, sure," Elizabeth muttered as Jessica bounced back to her own desk. But she smiled to herself anyway.

By three o'clock the pace in the newsroom was still fairly slow. Elizabeth joined Seth at his desk to review some notes they were coordinating for an upcoming series of articles.

"I need some coffee, or I'll fall asleep," Seth said after a few minutes. He pushed himself up from his desk and headed for the elevator. There was a coffee shop on the main floor of the Western Building. "Want some?" he called over his shoulder.

Elizabeth shook her head. "No, thanks. Seth!" she added as his telephone rang.

"Get it for me, will you?"

Elizabeth reached for the receiver. "Hello, newsroom."

"This is a friend calling." The voice was a whisper, strange and sexless.

Elizabeth put her hand over the receiver and whispered loudly, "Seth, come back!"

Puzzled, Seth returned as Elizabeth said, "Can I help you?"

"I wanted to let you know—there's a bomb."

Elizabeth's eyebrows shot up, and she waved Seth frantically to pick up the extension on the next desk. "What—where?" she gasped. Her heart began pounding with a wild mixture of fear and exhilaration. It was Redman. It had to be. And she was talking to him!

"Where's the bomb?" she repeated so that Seth would know what they were talking about.

Redman's laugh was cheerful, but there was an unmistakable edge of madness in it. "Somewhere where there are plenty of folks, that's where."

Beside her, Seth was scribbling hastily on a pad. He held the pad out to her: *Keep him on the phone.* When Elizabeth nodded, he hung up and using another line, dialed a number.

"Well, you probably want to tell me exactly where, right? Or else you wouldn't have called." Elizabeth managed to keep her voice level and calm, but her thoughts were spinning. She could hear Seth at the next desk, speaking to the police.

Redman sighed. "Maybe I will, maybe I won't. But you sound like a nice lady, so I'll tell you."

Elizabeth gestured quickly to Seth and mouthed, "He's going to tell me." The reporter stood by her, staring intently at the phone against her ear.

"Where is it?" she coaxed.

"Valley Cinema. But don't worry. It'll go off before you can get there."

Jessica.

To Elizabeth it seemed as though the world had frozen. She could see her sister's laughing face and hear her chattering about sneaking off to the movies.

"Liz!" Seth shook her, but she couldn't speak.

"Where is it?" he shouted at her.

The phone line clicked silent. Elizabeth struggled for breath.

"Liz! Where's the bomb?"

Like someone rising up through deep water, Elizabeth gradually focused on Seth's face. Then she shook herself. She had to think fast. "It's at the Valley Cinema," she announced.

Seth grabbed the phone and slammed it down. "Come on!" He took a camera from the lower drawer of his desk and slung it over his shoulder.

Her heart pounding wildly, Elizabeth stumbled after him. Somehow she managed to follow him out into the parking garage and climb into his car. In minutes they were racing through town. Elizabeth was so frightened that she couldn't think, let alone speak, and Seth was too busy dodging traffic to say anything, either. As they approached the theater, they heard the wail of police sirens behind them.

"My God! Look!"

Elizabeth followed Seth's pointing finger as the car screeched to a halt. People were streaming out of the theater, pushing, shoving, and shouting. It was pure chaos.

Seth was out of the car in an instant, rushing forward with his camera clicking. Elizabeth followed him, searching the crowd for her sister.

The moment the manager stopped *Terror in the Subway* and asked everyone to exit the theater, Jessica knew it was a bomb. She grabbed Lila's arm in a viselike grip.

"Lila!" she hissed. People around them began pushing clumsily out into the aisles and talking in loud voices. "It's that psycho! Redman!"

"I know, I know." Lila yanked her arm free and sidestepped out of the row ahead of Jessica.

"Please keep calm, everyone!" The manager tried to shout above the noise. "Don't panic!"

A woman screamed. "It's a fire! Patty? Patty, where are you?"

"Let me out of here!"

"Stop shoving!"

"Get out of my way!"

"It's not a fire! Please don't panic!"

Jessica stumbled against someone and stopped.

The line was stuck. Lila was ahead and to the right, but Jessica couldn't reach her. She was surrounded by noise and confusion, and for a split second Jessica was afraid she would be trampled by the people pushing behind her. Then the crowd surged forward again toward the exit doors, and Jessica was swept along. In a moment she was outside, blinking in the bright sunlight.

"Jessica?"

She whirled around at the sound of her twin's voice. "Liz!"

Elizabeth rushed up to her and enveloped her in a tight bear hug. "Are you all right?" Elizabeth asked. "It's a bomb scare. I think it's Donald Redman."

Nodding, Jessica scanned the crowd. The stores on either side of the theater had been evacuated, too. Police swarmed all over the parking lot, and people were milling around in complete turmoil. Sirens wailed, and officers with megaphones were trying to keep the terrified mob under control.

"Yeah, it was wild inside." Jessica glanced back at her sister, suddenly surprised. "How'd you get here so fast?"

"Redman called the newspaper office to make the bomb threat," Elizabeth explained. "I took the call, and Seth called the police. Then we came right over."

A sudden flush of anxiety colored Jessica's cheeks. "Do you think he saw me? Seth?"

"I doubt it," her sister said. "He's too busy taking pictures and getting the story."

Jessica breathed a sigh of relief. She didn't want anyone at the paper to know she was playing hooky. "Good. I think I'll go stand somewhere out of sight, though. I have to find Lila."

"OK." Elizabeth looked at her twin anxiously. "But come back to the office later."

"Sure, Liz. See you." Jessica turned and dodged through the crowd.

After a few minutes of searching, Jessica came across a small group of Sweet Valley High students standing together. Lila was with them, and so was Bruce Patman.

"Were you guys all at the movie?" Jessica asked.

Maria Santelli and Sandra Bacon shook their heads. "We were shopping."

"We were at the movie," Neil Freemount said. He was standing near Bruce. "I can't believe they cut it right at the part where the drones were starting to climb up through the sewers."

"Yeah, that was such a gyp," Lila agreed wryly. She scowled in the direction of police officers who were talking in a huddle. "What's going on, anyway? Is there a bomb or not?"

Jessica saw Seth Miller elbow his way toward

the police, just as a uniformed man in bomb squad gear came out of the building, holding something. Intrigued, Jessica stood on tiptoe and craned her neck to see better. Seth was scribbling rapidly in his notebook, but he stopped to take a picture of what the policeman was carrying. With a red ribbon and a tag on it, it looked like a Christmas present and was about the size of a typewriter. Only the businesslike air of the policemen showed how serious it was.

"That's no bomb," Bruce announced in a superior, know-it-all tone. "The cops wouldn't be standing there talking about their pension fund if it was real."

Lila gave Bruce a withering look. "Give me a break. Since when are you such an expert?"

"Hey, I'm good at a lot of things." Bruce smirked at Lila, who turned her back on him.

While Jessica watched, Seth nodded, flipped his notebook shut, and then hurried back to the parking lot. An excited buzz went up from the crowd as the police carried the object to a waiting police van and stowed it inside. For several minutes Jessica and her friends stood around, waiting for a signal to go back inside or to leave. Everyone traded opinions on what was happening, but no one knew for sure.

"Jessica!" Elizabeth's voice drifted through the noise to her sister.

"Liz! Over here!" Jessica called back. "Did you find out anything?" she asked when Elizabeth was by her side.

"Yeah," Elizabeth gasped. She caught her breath while everyone crowded around her. "Seth got a good look at it. It's a fake bomb. The tag on it says, 'Got ya. See you next time, kids.' Isn't that sick?"

Jessica's eyes lit up. "Was it Redman?"

"That's what it looks like."

"What does it mean, though?" Neil asked.

Elizabeth shook her head. "They aren't sure. They think it was a warning and that he might do it again for real."

"Wow." Impressed, Jessica looked back at the theater. Shaking her head, she walked a few paces away while the others plied Elizabeth with more questions. This had to be the most exciting thing that had happened in Sweet Valley in a long time, Jessica decided.

Hearing Elizabeth and Bruce in conversation, Jessica looked back just as Elizabeth smiled and waved goodbye to Bruce.

A spark of anger flared up in Jessica. She couldn't stand to see the smug look on Bruce's face; he really thought that Elizabeth cared about him! Scowling fiercely, Jessica faced Bruce, her hands on her hips.

"Listen, Bruce."

He cocked his eyebrows. "Yesssss?"

"You've got the wrong idea about Liz, you know." She curled her lip scornfully. "She doesn't really like you, she just thinks you're dying. That's why she's being so nice to you lately."

Bruce stared at her for a moment and then let out an astonished laugh. "Why does she think that?"

"It doesn't matter why," Jessica said, waving away the reason. "But she thinks you're terminally ill. Now you know, so you can forget trying to be Mr. Magnificent."

Bruce gave her a devilish grin. "I don't know, Jess. It seems like an interesting scenario to me."

Jessica narrowed her eyes in suspicion. "What do you mean?"

"Nothing. See you around, Wakefield." Bruce strolled away, chuckling.

Jessica stared at his back, her anger returning. She had assumed Bruce would back off once he knew why Elizabeth was being so nice. After all, the truth wasn't flattering to Bruce's ego. But it didn't appear he was offended—quite the contrary.

Nine

That evening Elizabeth was deeply absorbed in *Beginner's Guide to Occultism* when the phone rang. Since she was baby-sitting for Max, and he was sleeping, she jumped up immediately to answer it.

"Hello? Bartel residence."

There was no answer.

Elizabeth frowned. "Hello?"

She heard the dial tone before she finished the word. Swallowing hard, Elizabeth carefully replaced the receiver and stared at the phone. That was the second hang-up call she had gotten at the Bartels'. What made it so disturbing was that she had been getting hang-up calls at home, too.

Can the Ouija board be right? she asked herself nervously. *Is someone trying to contact me?*

Vaguely worried, Elizabeth curled up on the couch again and tried to concentrate on her book. So many things had happened with the Ouija board in the last week that she had to try to make sense of it all. Her mind was whirling with facts, theories, and strange occurrences.

Sighing, she realized she had just read the same paragraph for the third time. She lowered the book to her lap and looked across the living room. The house was quiet, and Elizabeth felt extremely isolated.

"Maybe there's something on TV." She spoke out loud, to make herself feel less alone, and reached for the remote control. Just as she clicked on the set, though, the phone rang again.

She stared, afraid to answer it. But when it rang again, she knew she couldn't let it wake up Max.

"H-hello?" she stammered as she lifted the receiver.

"Hi, Liz? It's Bruce."

Elizabeth's shoulders sagged with relief. There was nothing supernatural about Bruce calling her. She had mentioned to him at the mall that she would be baby-sitting for Max Bartel that night. He must have found the Bartels' number in the phone book.

Leaning back on the couch, she cradled the receiver against her shoulder. "Hi, what's up?"

"Nothing, really. I just . . ." His voice trailed off.

"Just what, Bruce?" Elizabeth was immediately concerned. "Are you all right?"

Bruce sighed into the telephone. "I guess. Maybe I'm just kind of depressed. *You* know," he added in a meaningful tone.

Any doubts that Elizabeth still had about Bruce being sick vanished instantly. She sat up straighter. "Try not to think about it," she said sympathetically. "Don't let it get to you."

"I try, but it's hard."

She nodded. "Just think positive thoughts," she said in her most sincere, encouraging voice. "There's a lot of proof that positive thinking actually helps."

"Maybe. But it's so hard alone. I just sit here by myself and think about it." Bruce was silent for a moment. "You can always make me feel better, though. Maybe I could come over?"

Elizabeth was torn. On the one hand, she really wanted to help Bruce, especially now that he was willing to talk about his problem. But on the other hand, she knew it was wrong to invite anyone over while she was baby-sitting. Her sense of responsibility just wouldn't let her do it.

Regretfully she said, "I'm sorry, Bruce. I really can't have you over. Mrs. Bartel wouldn't like it."

"I wouldn't have to stay very long. Just a few minutes," he coaxed.

"No," Elizabeth said. "I really am sorry, though. Do you want to have lunch together tomorrow? I'd really like to help if I can."

Bruce laughed gently. "You'd help me if you let me come over."

"Bruce, I just can't."

Elizabeth was partly touched and partly frustrated by his persistence. For a brief moment she toyed with the idea of relenting and letting him come over. But even as she considered it, she reminded herself it would be wrong. She just couldn't do it.

"Well, if you have to be so stubborn—"

"I'm not trying to be mean," Elizabeth broke in anxiously. "Really. It just wouldn't be right without asking Mrs. Bartel first. That's all. If it wasn't for that, you know I'd say yes."

Bruce sighed again. "I guess I understand."

"Good. I'm really sorry."

"Well, goodbye."

The forlorn sound in his voice tugged at Elizabeth's heart. "Bye," she whispered. Then she hung up and sat staring off into space. She kept thinking about Bruce and about the correct predictions from the Ouija board. Tired and confused, she tried to forget everything by focusing on the television show.

When the doorbell rang half an hour later, she let out a groan. "Bruce," she muttered, half laughing. "I can't believe you."

Shaking her head, she went to the door. It was a wooden door, with three small windows at the top. Standing on tiptoe, she looked out. It wasn't Bruce, however. It was a young, dark-haired man with glasses.

Elizabeth slipped the chain into the slot and opened the door a crack. "Yes?"

The man jumped slightly, as though startled, and tried to look past her into the house. He recovered his poise quickly. "Hi. Is Elsa home?"

"I'm sorry. She's out right now." Elizabeth cautiously avoided saying how long Elsa would be gone. "Can I tell her you stopped by?"

"Oh, well . . ."

He glanced over his shoulder once, then looked back. Elizabeth noticed that he had a few days worth of whiskers, but otherwise he was nice-looking, about Elsa's age. He wore the kind of wire-rimmed glasses Elizabeth liked.

"You see, I'm an old college friend of Elsa's, and I wanted to surprise her. I'm only in town till tomorrow, so I'll stop by in the morning," he said.

Still holding the door, Elizabeth nodded. "OK, I'll tell her," she agreed with a polite smile.

He nodded. "Fine. Umm"—he looked at her intently—"I know this sounds funny, but what's your name?"

Elizabeth hesitated. It bothered her to have strangers ask questions when she was baby-sitting.

Seeing her uneasiness, the man flashed a brief smile. "It's just that you look so much like someone I—used to know," he explained. He continued to stare at her.

"Oh, I—" Elizabeth's voice faltered. She felt uncomfortable and wished he would leave. "I'll tell Mrs. Bartel you were here," she said as firmly as she could and started to close the door.

The man's smile instantly disappeared. "OK. Thanks a lot," he said in a monotone. He turned and walked down the steps. The darkness quickly swallowed him.

Still slightly unsettled, Elizabeth locked the door and wandered back to the couch. She wrote on the message pad by the phone, "Old friend will stop by tomorrow to see you." Then she curled up to watch the last half of a sitcom.

Fifteen minutes later the doorbell rang again.

"*Now* what?" she gasped, jumping to her feet.

She couldn't remember a busier night of baby-sitting.

One glance through the windows showed her it *was* Bruce this time. Repressing a sigh, she opened the door and gave him a long, silent look.

"Hi," he said. "Guess who?"

"Bruce, you really shouldn't have come."

He gave her a sheepish little-boy smile and tossed his dark hair out of his eyes. "Sorry. I had to talk to you, though."

Elizabeth didn't want to argue, so she stepped aside and ushered him in. She didn't know whether to be angry with him or flattered that he was so eager to see her. "All right. But only for a few minutes, Bruce. I mean it."

"No problem." Bruce put his hands in his pockets and turned around, looking at the living room. "Nice place. Can I sit down, or don't I have time for that?"

Elizabeth couldn't help laughing. "Go ahead." She sat down on the couch, folded her legs underneath her, and gave him a wry smile. "So, anyway . . ."

"Anyway." Bruce grinned at her, a questioning light in his eyes as he sat down on the couch beside her. But then his smile faded, and he shook his head. "I was just feeling depressed, you know? Sometimes I don't know why I keep trying to act like nothing's wrong."

"It's not such a bad idea, though," Elizabeth replied. She was filled with concern and sympathy again, as she remembered *why* Bruce had come over. "Just keep living exactly the way you always have. Don't let this change you or stop you from doing what you like."

Bruce nodded earnestly and edged closer to her. "I know what you mean," he said, looking deep into her eyes. "But sometimes . . ." He held her gaze steadily.

For a moment Elizabeth stared back at him. It was so hard to accept the fact that he was sick, but her heart gave a painful lurch, and she reached impulsively for his hand.

"Bruce, I'm so sorry," she said in a choked voice.

"Liz, you don't know what it's like."

She pressed her lips together to keep them from trembling. Bruce looked so desolate, so vulnerable.

Suddenly Elizabeth had a crazy feeling he was about to kiss her. Even though she knew she was imagining it, she sat back and tried to change the mood.

"How about lunch tomorrow?" she suggested in a brisk, cheerful voice.

Bruce kept his eyes on her for another long

moment, and then he sat back, too. "Sure, that would be great."

"Well," she continued, rising to her feet, "I hate to do this to you, but you'd better go now."

"You're sure?" Bruce leaned back and folded his arms across his chest. The look he sent her was unreadable.

Elizabeth smiled apologetically, but she gave him a firm nod. "Definitely." She stood up.

"OK. I know when to back off," he said softly. Bruce pushed himself off the couch and stood close beside her. "Bye."

Stepping back a pace, Elizabeth looked up into his eyes. "Bye. See you tomorrow."

They stood staring at each other for the space of several heartbeats. Then the phone rang. Startled, Elizabeth broke away from Bruce's mesmerizing gaze.

"Hello?" There was nothing but silence at the other end of the line. Elizabeth's pulse jumped. *"Hello?"*

"Who was that?" Bruce asked as she hung up.

Elizabeth took a deep breath. She didn't want to let on how much it disturbed her. "Nobody. I guess it's just someone's idea of a joke," she said with an attempt at lightness. She led him to the door.

"Well, I'll see you tomorrow." Bruce paused on

the threshold and looked at her for another long moment. "Bye."

When she shut the door behind him, Elizabeth let out a sigh of relief. The atmosphere had gotten very electric, and it bothered her. She knew Bruce could easily confuse gratitude toward her for something deeper. Yet she didn't want to hurt his feelings by reminding him that she was just a friend.

"I wish Jeffrey would come home," she muttered aloud as she sank onto the couch again. "Things have been getting too much to handle lately."

She shook her head. Too many things *had* been happening, what with the Ouija board turning out to be legitimate, a psychotic bomber on the loose, and finding out that Bruce was so sick. And now she was getting strange hang-up calls. Somehow she was sure that when Jeffrey came back from camp, everything would return to normal.

And I can't wait for things to be normal again, she added silently.

Ten

After dinner on Wednesday, it was Jessica's turn to clean up and load the dishwasher. Since the twins' mother worked full-time, everyone shared the housework. But Jessica still grumbled every time she had to wash a dirty saucepan. Out on the patio, her parents and Steven were relaxing and talking. Elizabeth was reading a magazine at the kitchen table. Jessica was standing at the sink, scowling at the pans soaking in the sink and complaining to herself, when the phone rang.

A quick glance at the clock told her it was Lila's scheduled hang-up call. She cleared her throat. "Liz, would you get that? My hands are all soapy."

Elizabeth put down her magazine and reached for the wall telephone. "Hello?"

At the sink Jessica watched her sister from the corner of her eye. Lila had told Jessica exactly when she would be making the "urgent message" calls from the "other side" that the Ouija board had predicted. That way, Jessica could make sure Elizabeth answered the phone.

"Hello?"

Elizabeth's expression went from happy to upset. Quickly she hung up the phone, then stood staring blankly into space.

The worried look in her twin's eyes sent a pang of guilt rippling through Jessica. She didn't know why Lila was so determined to keep up the mysterious message routine, but Jessica was beginning to feel their hoax wasn't very funny anymore.

"Who was that?" she asked halfheartedly. She had lost the spirit of the game, but she had to keep up the act for Lila's sake.

Elizabeth shook her head and sat back down at the table. Her voice was subdued. "Nobody. That's about the sixth or seventh time that someone's hung up on me when I answered the phone. It even happened a few times when I was at the Bartels'."

"Oh. That's funny."

Jessica looked studiously at the sinkful of pots and pans again. It wasn't funny. What had started out as a harmless joke was getting completely out of hand. And what made it worse was that Bruce was spending even more time with Elizabeth than ever. Jessica knew her twin had had lunch with him the day before, and he had called Elizabeth after dinner, too.

She wrinkled her nose as a new idea hatched in her mind. Could Bruce actually be falling for her sister? It was an appalling thought, she decided, but possibly true. Normally Bruce didn't spend so much time chasing after a girl who didn't "give something back." He usually went for the more exciting type. But it couldn't be denied that Bruce was concentrating his attention on Elizabeth to an amazing degree, and all Elizabeth was doing was being her usual sweet, friendly self.

One thing Jessica was sure of, though, was that it wasn't fair to Elizabeth to let her keep thinking Bruce was ill. If she knew Bruce was healthy, Elizabeth wouldn't have two words to say to him. And, in Jessica's opinion, it was time to do something about it.

Jessica cleared her throat. "Liz? I thought I should tell—"

A knock on the back door cut her off.

"Hang on—I'll get it," said her sister.

Elizabeth jumped up and crossed the kitchen while Jessica turned back to scowl at the dirty pots and pans again. She didn't know which was worse, betraying her friend or betraying her twin. Behind her, she heard the all-too-familiar voice that made her wince.

"Hey, Jessica," Bruce said, following Elizabeth inside. "How's it going?"

Darting him a chilly glance, Jessica scrubbed a pot and said nothing.

"How about something to drink?" Elizabeth offered.

Jessica frowned. Her sister was constantly looking after Bruce now, urging him to take it easy, bringing him treats to cheer him up. Her concern for his well-being was almost too much to tolerate.

"Bruce isn't thirsty," Jessica announced in a loud voice.

Her twin looked at her in surprise. "What?"

"I guess Jessica thinks I come over too much," Bruce said, his eyes gleaming with mischief as he looked at Jessica.

Elizabeth sent her a stern look that said, "Remember—he's sick, so we have to be nice to him." Disgusted, Jessica turned her back on both of them.

"So, what's the story with this school rally tonight, anyway?" Bruce asked. He sat down at the table and stretched out his long legs. "Are we supposed to go and show what good stu-

110

dents we are? Show we haven't forgotten about good ol' Sweet Valley High?"

Elizabeth laughed. "It's 'Be True to Your School' night at the football stadium, Bruce. I told you about it yesterday. The cheerleaders are holding it to get everyone back in the school spirit. Right, Jess?"

As co-captain of the cheerleading squad, Jessica had to participate in all school rallies. She didn't feel like going to the rally that night, though. She wasn't in a very cheerful mood. So she shrugged and grimaced. "Yeah. Big deal."

"Then I'm definitely going," Bruce said, grinning. He turned to Elizabeth. "Why don't I drive you?"

Jessica spoke up again firmly. "Cara's picking me up, so Liz can drive herself. But she *really* appreciates the offer, Bruce," she added in a sarcastic tone.

Elizabeth gave her another shocked, puzzled look. "Jessica!" Elizabeth turned to Bruce. "I don't know what's wrong with her," she apologized. "Maybe she didn't get her nap today."

"Ha-ha, Liz." Growing more irritated and guilt-ridden by the second, Jessica dried her hands and stomped out of the kitchen. Having Bruce around so much just underlined the fact that the Ouija board hoax had gone too far. As she reached the staircase, the doorbell rang. "What is this, anyway," she growled, "the bus station?"

With a stormy look in her eyes, Jessica yanked open the front door. Then her jaw dropped.

"Hi, Jess! Surprise!"

A tall blond boy with a deep tan was standing on the front step. Jessica stared at him and gulped.

"Jeffrey," she gasped, wide-eyed. "What are *you* doing here?"

He grinned, showing perfect white teeth. "I was going to stay at camp for the extra canoe trip, but at the last minute they had more counselors than they needed. So I got to come home early." He looked past her into the house. "Is Liz here? I wanted to surprise her."

A laugh bubbled up in Jessica's throat. "She'll definitely be surprised."

Glancing over Jeffrey's shoulder, she noticed that Bruce's black Porsche was parked in the shadows across the street. Jeffrey must not have spotted it. She nodded toward the back of the house. "Liz is in the kitchen."

"Great." Jeffrey walked past her and headed down the hall.

Jessica watched him for a minute and then smiled to herself. Now that Jeffrey was back, she didn't have to worry about Bruce Patman anymore. Her conscience was now perfectly clear. She tried to imagine the scene about to take place in the kitchen and let out a giggle. Then she ran up the stairs to get changed for the rally. Suddenly her mood was one hundred percent lighter.

"Was that the front door?" Bruce asked, putting down his glass.

Elizabeth nodded. "I think Jess got it." She leaned forward, her elbows propped up on the table, and looked earnestly at Bruce. "So, how do you feel today? Any better?"

"Oh, you know," he replied with a shrug. "Some days are easier than others."

Elizabeth shook her head. "I don't know how you do it." Sighing, she tilted her head to one side and gave Bruce a tender smile. "I think you're amazing, really."

Bruce smiled at her, but then his gaze shifted to a spot behind her, and his expression underwent a dramatic change. Curious, Elizabeth turned around.

"Jeffrey!" Stunned but happy, she jumped out of her chair and threw her arms around him. "What are you doing here?"

Jeffrey hugged her back, but his eyes were on Bruce. "I was finished early—I wanted to surprise you." His voice sounded stilted.

Elizabeth couldn't stop smiling, she was so glad to see him. But she could sense the undercurrent of tension around the kitchen table. She realized that Jeffrey must have overheard her compliment to Bruce, and immediately she saw how disappointing it must have been for Jeffrey to have planned a surprise for her and then have found her with another boy. He was the one who was surprised. She felt a surge of love and tenderness for him.

"I can't believe you're really here," Elizabeth breathed, her eyes like stars. She waved one hand toward Bruce. "We were just about to go to the spirit rally I told you about in my last letter. Now you can go, too." She tried to convey the fact that Bruce's presence was perfectly innocent.

"Sure, you can come, too," Bruce agreed. He gave Jeffrey a typically cocky grin and leaned back in his chair with his arms folded.

Jeffrey glanced from Bruce to Elizabeth and back again, looking as though he wanted to say something. His hurt and bewilderment was obvious in his green eyes.

It's not what you think, silly, Elizabeth told him silently. *But I can't tell you why Bruce is here. It's his secret, and I can't give it away.*

"So, anyway," she said, pulling her boyfriend

to a chair and sitting down next to him, "was this the big secret you were saving up for me?"

Jeffrey pulled his eyes away from Bruce and gave her a quick smile. "Right. I knew last week I might leave camp early, but I didn't want to say anything in case I was asked to stay."

"You sneak." Elizabeth grinned at him, communicating her love with her eyes.

There was an uncomfortable silence at the table, and Elizabeth began to feel strained. To change the subject, and the mood, she stood up briskly. "Why don't we go to the rally. It's starting in about half an hour."

"Sure," Bruce agreed. "We can go in my car."

"My car's bigger," Jeffrey pointed out, his voice pleasant but firm.

Bruce pretended to be surprised. "Oh, I just meant you could follow us."

"Since Jeffrey just got back, I'll go with him." Elizabeth stepped between the two boys. She could sense the rivalry between them and didn't know whether to feel flattered or annoyed. "We'll meet you there, OK, Bruce?"

He stared at her for a moment, then said, "Sure. Meet you there." Waving casually, he strolled across the kitchen and let himself out the back door.

Jeffrey spun around as soon as Bruce was gone. "What was that all—"

"It's nothing," Elizabeth cut in. She stood on her tiptoes and kissed him on the lips. "We're just friends, that's all. You know there could never be anything between Bruce and me," she added.

"So why's he here?"

Elizabeth bit her lip. She wasn't supposed to let on about Bruce's illness, so she couldn't explain that she was just being nice out of sympathy. Jeffrey would just have to trust her.

"I—can't tell you right now. He just comes over sometimes. There's nothing for you to get nervous about," she told him. "Really."

Wrapping his arms around her, Jeffrey looked down into her eyes. Gradually a reluctant smile spread across his face. "You're sure."

"Positive," she said.

"But you'll tell me about it later on, though, right?"

"I—" Elizabeth kissed him again to avoid answering. Before long, everyone would know about Bruce's condition. But until then, her lips were sealed. "I think we should get going."

Eleven

The football stadium was mobbed with students and parents by the time Elizabeth and Jeffrey arrived. They made their way slowly through the crowd, greeting friends they hadn't seen since school let out for the summer. "Chrome Dome" Cooper, the high school principal, was standing on a platform in the middle of the field, speaking through a microphone.

"Take your seats, everyone!" he called out in a hearty, jocular voice. "We've got a big program for you tonight!"

Wild applause broke out when everyone noticed Dana Larson heading for the stage. Dana was the lead singer for the school's best band, The Droids.

"Are The Droids playing tonight?" Jeffrey

asked. He took Elizabeth's hand as they maneuvered up through the packed stands.

"Yep. Isn't it fantastic?" Elizabeth replied over the noise from a thousand high school students, little brothers and sisters, parents and teachers.

A feeling of anticipation was in the air, and a roar went up from the stands as the cheerleaders jogged out onto the field. Elizabeth grinned with excitement as she sat down. She could see Jessica give the first few rows a dazzling smile.

"This is so great," Elizabeth said. She squeezed Jeffrey's hand and looked into his eyes. It was so wonderful to see him. She leaned forward to give him a quick kiss. "Aren't you glad you got back today?"

Jeffrey nodded. "Definitely."

Elizabeth detected a hint of tension in his voice. On the way over, she had filled him in on all the latest news, especially about the ongoing Donald Redman story. But she hadn't brought up the Ouija board business because it was too complicated and strange to get into on the way to school. And she hadn't told him why she was being so friendly to Bruce, either. She sensed that Jeffrey was hurt and mystified, but there was nothing she could do about it.

"Let's just have a good time," she suggested softly. Out on the field, the cheerleaders started rousing the crowd with a Sweet Valley High chant. "I'm really glad you're home."

"Me, too," Jeffrey murmured. "I missed you so much, Liz."

He slipped one arm around her shoulders and hugged her to him. But then he tensed. Bruce was making his way up the bleachers toward them. Bruce stopped every now and then to speak to someone in the stands, but there was no doubt he was planning to sit with them.

"Liz?" Jeffrey's jaw was clenched.

"Don't worry about it. Please?" She looked searchingly into his eyes. "Just trust me on this one and don't ask."

Jeffrey bit back a reply as Bruce seated himself on Elizabeth's other side.

"Howdy, folks," Bruce drawled. He jingled his car keys in his hand, as though to suggest he wasn't staying long. "It looks like they're really going all out to get the school spirit up."

"I'm surprised you even wanted to come," Jeffrey said in a slightly sarcastic tone. "This isn't your usual type of scene."

Bruce smiled crookedly and then pocketed his keys. "Maybe I've changed. You've been gone a long time. A lot can happen when you're away."

"Yeah, well, I'm back now." Jeffrey tightened

his arm around Elizabeth and gave Bruce a pointed look.

Elizabeth glanced from face to face, wondering if she should say anything about the ridiculous way they were behaving. On one hand, she felt flattered to have them vying for her attention. But on the other hand, she felt that Jeffrey, at least, should know better. After all, she had asked him to trust her. She wished he would simply have faith in her and relax.

As Elizabeth opened her mouth to change the conversation, the cheerleaders left the field, and Dana Larson took the microphone. "Hi, everyone!"

"Hi!" the crowd roared back, whistling and waving. An entire section of the stadium started stomping its feet in unison.

Dana lifted one arm over her head. She had a lot of stage presence and really knew how to turn an audience on. She waited for silence and then said in a deep voice, "This is a little event we do each summer. We call this gig 'Be True to Your School.' "

She was interrupted by another deafening wave of sound from the stands. The stadium was packed with people, and it looked like everyone was having a great time. Dana waited for the noise to die down a bit. Behind her, the other band members climbed up onto the stage and switched on their amps. Someone in the audience howled.

"So, just to make sure you don't forget what being in school is like," Dana continued, grinning, "we're going to play a song of ours called 'A-Plus.' "

The audience went wild as The Droids broke into one of their most popular numbers. Elizabeth, Jeffrey, and Bruce stood up with everyone else to cheer and clap, but even with all the excitement, Elizabeth noticed the two boys giving each other competitive looks. She stifled a sigh of exasperation as they all settled down again to listen.

"Are you thirsty, Liz?" Bruce asked. "I can go get us something to drink."

"I'll get it," Jeffrey cut in before Elizabeth could answer. He glared at Bruce and then switched his gaze to her. "Root beer?"

They were like two dogs circling around a tasty bone, Elizabeth thought. And she didn't like being a tasty bone. Elizabeth felt as if she was a prize for the winner, and that meant they weren't paying any attention to what she said or wanted. The more she thought about it, the more insulted she felt. She stood up abruptly and looked Jeffrey in the eye.

"Listen, I *am* thirsty, but I'd rather get something myself," she announced in a firm, no-argument voice. She edged out to the aisle and strode down the steps, shaking her head with annoyance.

Elizabeth gritted her teeth, trying not to lose her temper. She couldn't believe Jeffrey and Bruce were acting so childishly when there was absolutely no reason to. Maybe they just needed a chance to work off a little steam, and she didn't see why she needed to be there while they did it.

"Hi, Liz," called a group of friends.

She waved absently and smiled, but her mind was far away. She waltzed to the yawning passageway leading under the stands. The rhythmic, danceable music of The Droids followed her as she went down into the interior of the big stadium.

At the end of the short tunnel, the cool cement hallway stretched away on either side in a long curve. In each direction were offices, locker rooms, and rest rooms. People passed back and forth down the corridor, chatting and laughing. Elizabeth paused to get her bearings. It wasn't easy to tell where she was, because all the archways leading inside looked the same. After a moment's hesitation, she turned left.

Why do they have to act like jealous rivals? she asked herself as she walked along. *It's so dumb.*

Deep in thought, she stared at the floor as she walked. Just ahead of her, a door opened, and someone stepped out into the corridor. Elizabeth looked up to avoid a collision and saw it was Mr. Cooper, the principal. He was still holding on to the doorknob of the office door, and his face was drained of color.

"Mr. Cooper?" she asked, instantly concerned. He looked as though he were about to faint. "Mr. Cooper, are you all right?"

He gulped air and then pushed past her, running for the nearest tunnel out to the field. Startled and perplexed, Elizabeth stared after him. She started to follow.

As she rounded the curve, she saw another man hurrying in her direction. He looked up, and their eyes met as he rushed past.

Elizabeth stopped and turned to watch him. It was the same man who had come to Elsa Bartel's house two nights before, Elsa's college friend.

The shock of recognition seemed to catch up with the man after he had gone several paces beyond Elizabeth. His steps faltered, and he turned around to stare at her for a moment.

The same blue eyes behind the glasses, the same ruffled dark hair—it was definitely him, Elizabeth thought. Then as she watched, he hurried on and disappeared down another corridor.

Shrugging, Elizabeth turned and followed Dana's amplified voice back toward the football field. But another voice came back in her memory. *"I'm only in town till tomorrow, so I'll stop by in the morning."*

Elizabeth slowed down, frowned, and looked over her shoulder again. "Why would he say . . . ?"

Then she hurried off in the direction Mr. Cooper had gone. As she rushed outside, she heard Dana and the rest of The Droids come to a sudden halt in mid-song. A jangled chord twanged in the void, and a grumble of protest went up from the bleachers.

"Attention, everyone!" Elizabeth could see Mr. Cooper onstage. He was holding Dana's microphone. Even from a distance Elizabeth could see he was nervous. "We have to cancel the program. Please exit the stadium immediately!"

Beside Elizabeth, a girl standing with her boyfriend let out a piercing scream. "It's another bomb!" she shrieked, eyes wide with fear.

"A bomb!" The word spread through the stands like wildfire.

Instantly everyone in the stadium was up and pressing toward the exits. The air was filled with screams and shouts, and Elizabeth was pushed and knocked aside by people blindly running for safety. Elizabeth saw the happy, cheerful crowd change to a panicked mob. Terrified, she flattened herself against the wall, searching anxiously for a familiar face while people rushed past her.

"Please don't run!" Mr. Cooper's voice was barely audible above the screams and yells. "Please stay calm!"

"Gerry! Where are you?"

"I left my purse behind!"

"Ow! Don't push me!"

"Move! Move! Get going!"

Elizabeth's pulse hammered in her ears. The mob was dangerous, she realized in shock. There was no way to slow them down or stop them, and someone was bound to be hurt. The first person who fell would be trampled.

Jeffrey and Bruce! she suddenly thought.

"Oh, no," she moaned. All she could think about was finding her friends. Desperate, she began struggling against the current, forcing her way back to the bleachers to find them.

"Are you crazy?"

"You're going the wrong way!"

Angry shouts blasted in her ears, but Elizabeth ignored them. Panting, she dragged herself out of the tunnel into the daylight of the stadium again and stopped in horrified amazement.

The stadium was a milling, swirling mass of people, all trying to squeeze through the tunnels and out the exits. A flood of police officers was pouring in, trying to keep the mob under control, but no one was paying any attention. Onstage, a group of police huddled around Mr. Cooper, and a detachment broke away, heading for the stadium interior.

A tall, attractive man hurried past Elizabeth. She shouted out in recognition. "Mr. Collins! Wait!"

Her English teacher turned, a distracted, impatient expression on his face. But when he saw Elizabeth, he strode to her side. "Liz, get out of here, now!"

"Is it Redman?" she gasped.

Roger Collins drew his breath in sharply and nodded. "Yes. He called and identified himself. He also called the police. He says there's a bomb in here somewhere." Mr. Collins took her arm. "Now, come on. You're getting out of here."

They watched the rushing crowd for a moment. The last frightened group of spectators from that section of the stadium pushed into the tunnel and disappeared. When the way was clear, Mr. Collins pulled Elizabeth after him down the tunnel and into the corridor.

"Come on," he ordered, heading after the receding mob.

Elizabeth let out a tiny, frightened sob. "Jeffrey and Bruce are still—"

"Liz." Mr. Collins looked at her, and his stern expression softened slightly. "They're out already, you can be sure of it," he told her.

Trying to be brave, Elizabeth nodded. Then around the bend came a troop of policemen in bomb squad gear. They stopped at a door marked Lost and Found and fanned out. The leader of the group nodded to his partner and tested the doorknob. Gasping, Mr. Collins pushed Elizabeth behind him, shielding her.

Elizabeth felt a strange mixture of horror and fascination as she peered around Mr. Collins to watch the bomb experts file into the room. Short, terse commands were barked from inside the room, and seconds later the leader emerged, carrying a package tied in red ribbon.

"Another fake," he announced in clipped tones. He examined the bundle. "He emptied the sticks, but they're real."

"Real dynamite?" Elizabeth whispered, looking up at Mr. Collins.

He nodded. "That's what it looks like. He must have emptied the TNT out of them, but it proves he's got access to the real thing."

Elizabeth looked back at the policemen in shock. At the same moment they noticed her and Mr. Collins. One of them came striding forward.

"Clear the area, folks. There may be more."

"Is there a note this time?" Elizabeth couldn't help asking. "Was it Redman?"

The officer looked at her in silence for a moment, then nodded once. "Yeah. It's Redman, all right." He jerked his head toward the exit. "Now get going."

"Thanks, Officer," Mr. Collins said. "Come on, Liz."

As they hurried down the corridor, Elizabeth's mind raced ahead. Was Redman getting his revenge for being expelled from school? Did his paranoid mind hold Sweet Valley High responsible for his problems? Was it because of the taunting and the insults from the football clique?

"What does he want?" she asked out loud.

Beside her, Mr. Collins shook his head. "Who knows what goes on in a twisted mind? I didn't start teaching here until long after he left, but a few people remember him." The teacher shook his head and frowned. "Brilliant, but completely out of control."

Completely out of control. Elizabeth shivered. Who could tell what would satisfy Redman's thirst for vengeance? Would he continue to play cat and mouse with fake bombs? Or would the next one be real?

Elizabeth felt more frightened now than she had at the height of the pandemonium. Knowing they were at the mercy of a brilliant but unbalanced mind was almost worse than being in physical danger from a panicked mob. At least a fleeing mob was predictable. Redman wasn't.

When she and Mr. Collins emerged into the parking lot, it took Elizabeth a moment to catch her breath. The milling crowd was quieter, less like a herd of stampeding animals. An air of nervous expectation hung over the group. Mr. Collins gave Elizabeth a quick, reassuring smile, then headed for Mr. Cooper.

"Liz!"

She whirled around at the sound of her name. Huddled in a group were her sister, Jeffrey, Bruce, and several of their friends. Dangerously close to tears, Elizabeth rushed to them. Jessica wrapped her in a tight hug, and Jeffrey threw his arms around them both.

"I couldn't find you guys!" Elizabeth choked, overcome with emotion. Seeing people she loved after the chaos inside was an overwhelming relief. She took a deep, steadying breath and then tried to answer all their questions.

Afterward, as she and Jeffrey were driving home, Elizabeth couldn't get Redman out of her mind. To elude the police for so long and to plant fake bombs in such an obvious way—he had to be incredibly clever and devious.

She sighed and slumped deeper in the seat.

At the wheel, Jeffrey glanced at her and gave her a thin, worried smile. "Are you sure you're OK?"

"Yeah," Elizabeth whispered. She tried to muster a confident smile. "I'm fine."

Jeffrey reached for her hand but didn't speak. Feeling subdued, Elizabeth scooted closer to him and rested her head on his shoulder. All the joy of Jeffrey's homecoming had evaporated. All she could think of was: *When will Redman strike again?*

Twelve

On Thursday morning Jessica waited until Elizabeth was in the shower, and then she dialed Lila's number. She had been stewing about something since the previous evening and wanted to get it off her chest.

"Hey, Lila?"

"Jessica?" Lila sounded groggy and confused. Her voice cracked sleepily as she said, "What time is it?"

"Eight o'clock. Listen, I—"

"Eight o'clock? You're calling me at eight o'clock in the morning? This better be major."

Jessica rummaged through her closet, dragging the phone with her. As long as she had to wake up early in the summer, Lila might as well wake up too. "It is. Listen, about those phony phone calls to Liz? Cut it out, OK?"

She pulled a skirt off its hanger. "It's not funny anymore."

"Huh?" There was a rustling sound, as though Lila were wrestling with her sheets and bedspread. "I only did it a few times, Jess. Lighten up."

"A few times? You're even doing it when she baby-sits," Jessica corrected sharply.

Lila gasped. "I am not! You don't have to accuse me of every little prank phone call that gets made in the world, you know."

Jessica held the phone against her ear with her shoulder while she stepped into the skirt. She frowned. "You didn't make any hang-up calls to her at Mrs. Bartel's house?"

"No! Geez, give me a break!" Lila sounded peeved.

"Oh." Sitting down on the edge of the bed, Jessica looked off into space for a moment.

"Is that the major thing you woke me up for?" Lila went on irritably.

"Yeah. Well, sorry. Talk to you later."

"Yeah, sure," Lila grumbled. "Bye."

Jessica hung up the phone. She was puzzled. If it wasn't Lila who kept making hang-up calls to Liz, who was it?

When Elizabeth came down to breakfast, she found her entire family in a somber mood. The radio was tuned in to the local news station, and everyone sat silently, sipping coffee and listening to the latest bulletin on the near-riot at the football stadium the evening before.

"Good morning," she said, joining them.

Her mother gave her a faint smile but kept listening to the radio. Alice and Ned Wakefield had been shocked when the twins had come home from the stadium and told them of their horrifying experience.

"And in a related story," said the announcer, "police say escaped hospital patient Donald Redman also left his calling card at the county airport last night. Security guards received an anonymous tip, possibly from the wanted man himself, directing them to a suitcase in the Lost and Found. Investigation showed it to contain another fake bomb. A police spokesman is quoted as saying, 'At this time, we're assuming it's Redman again.' "

"This is too much!" Ned Wakefield exploded. He stood up and stalked across the kitchen to pour himself another cup of coffee.

Elizabeth met her twin's eyes over the table, but neither of them said a word. Steven pushed his spoon around in his cereal, his face gloomy.

"Police Commissioner Dreyfus told WSVK at a news conference early this morning 'The department is on full alert at this time. We are utilizing all of our available resources to apprehend the suspect and put an end to his campaign of terrorism,' " the news announcer continued. "Mark Nowicki, head of the Neighborhood Action Branch, or NAB, tells WSVK news that tempers are growing short in the city's residential districts. 'If the police can't catch that maniac, we citizens will have to defend ourselves,' Nowicki told our reporter."

"Great. That's all we need," muttered Mr. Wakefield. He let his breath out heavily and shook his head. "This is the type of situation that leads to vigilante justice."

"And that's not justice at all," Mrs. Wakefield pointed out grimly. "I say let the police handle it. They're trained to deal with this sort of thing."

Jessica let out an angry sigh. "But what if the police can't get him?" she demanded. Her blue-green eyes were wide with indignation. "I mean, so far they've been unable to track him down. Are they that incompetent?"

"Yeah," Steven agreed. He frowned. "It's hard to believe no one has seen the guy. His picture's been in the paper every single day since he took off from the nuthouse."

Jessica nodded emphatically. "Right. It's not like this is L.A. or New York. Sweet Valley is just a small town. You'd think someone would've seen him."

Elizabeth looked at her brother intently. His words triggered something in her mind, something lingering just at the brink of her memory. For some reason she was sure it was important, but it slipped away before she could grab it. Troubled, she looked down at her plate and said nothing.

Her father's expression was thoughtful. Clearly his lawyer's mind was working on the situation. He nodded. "That's true, Steve," he said. "But anyone as smart as Redman seems to be can change his appearance quite easily. You'd be surprised how different a person can look just by changing his hair or his posture. I've even seen cases in court where a suspect speaking with a different accent can throw a witness completely off track."

"I still think the police are a bunch of dopes," Jessica muttered.

"Jessica!" Mrs. Wakefield frowned but didn't say anything more.

Elizabeth didn't join in the conversation. Having the journalist's knack of seeing both sides of the issue, she sympathized with the neighborhood watch groups because they were frightened and felt powerless, but at the same time she knew the police were probably doing everything they could. However, when all was said and done, Redman was still on the loose.

"I'm afraid this situation is really building up," Mrs. Wakefield said in a serious tone. Her blue eyes were sad and anxious. "Sooner or later, something is just going to explode."

Jessica snorted. "You got that right, Mom."

"I meant—"

"We know what you meant, honey," Ned Wakefield broke in. He looked at his wife sorrowfully. "But I think Jessica's right, too. Sooner or later, Redman is going to start using the real thing."

Her father's words haunted Elizabeth all the way to the newspaper office. She couldn't get the scene at the stadium out of her mind, either. She could still hear the screams and see the shoving, chaotic crowd.

If that's the kind of panic you get with a fake bomb, what's going to happen when there's a real one? she asked herself. The possibilities were too awful to contemplate. Sweet Valley was in a state of terror.

Deep in thought, she sat down at her desk with a copy of the day's paper. While she read the "Stadium Scare" article, she picked up a pencil and began tapping it nervously against her palm. She couldn't shake the feeling that there was something she should figure out. But

136

she didn't know what it was, and it worried her more and more. Redman's picture stared at her from the middle of the front page.

Elizabeth bounced the eraser end of her pencil on his picture, and then, without thinking, she flipped the pencil over and shaded in the light-colored hair. The man's appearance began to change subtly under the rapid pencil strokes. Then, with her fingertip, Elizabeth smudged the newspaper ink around his cheeks and chin. Her heart pounded in her ears like a hammer as she took in the effect. Almost against her will, she carefully drew a pair of glasses on the picture and darkened the razor stubble on the upper lip. Then her hand faltered to a stop.

A cold prickle of fear crawled up her spine. Staring back at her from the newspaper page was Elsa Bartel's college friend, the same man she had seen at the football stadium just before the bomb alert! Elizabeth sat frozen in her chair. She couldn't hear or see anything going on in the office. All her attention was riveted to the face looking up at her. It was Redman in disguise.

Elizabeth's hand instinctively reached for the telephone to call the police. But before she punched in the emergency number, she hesitated. She hung up the phone.

For a moment Elizabeth stared at the picture

again. *Am I sure?* she asked herself. *Am I absolutely positive it's him?*

She raised her eyes and glanced around the newsroom. Reporters sat at their desks and computer terminals, or talked on the phone and paged through notes. Before making an accusation, she realized, she should check out her suspicions as thoroughly as she could. She imagined what would happen if she sent the police after an innocent man. With the mood Sweet Valley was in at the moment, a case of mistaken identity could cause a riot.

Squaring her shoulders, Elizabeth took her shoulder bag out of a drawer, opened it, and pulled out her phone book. Thumbing through it, she found the number she wanted. She pulled the phone toward her again, thought a moment, and then punched in Elsa Bartel's office number. She waited, hearing the ring, and stared at the photograph again.

"Good morning. Allied Equity Systems. Can I help you?" The monotonous voice caught Elizabeth off guard.

"I'd like to speak to Elsa Bartel, please," Elizabeth said when she jerked her attention back to the phone. "It's Elizabeth Wakefield calling."

"One moment, please."

Elizabeth stared sightlessly across the office. Now that she was about to speak to Elsa, she realized what a horrible question she was about to ask.

"Hello, Liz? Is that you?"

"Oh—hi, Mrs. Bartel," Elizabeth stammered. She cleared her throat uncomfortably, not knowing how to begin.

"What can I do for you, Liz?" Elsa sounded polite but puzzled. "A problem about sitting?"

Elizabeth shook her head, even though she knew the woman couldn't see her. Lowering her voice, she said, "No—it's not that. I wanted to ask you—about—"

There was a pause. Then Elsa prompted her. "What, Liz? Ask me what?"

Elizabeth closed her eyes for a moment. It was so difficult to ask. "Did your friend ever come by the other day? The one who wanted to surprise you?"

"Yes," Elsa replied. Her voice held a note of wariness. Or was it simply bewilderment? Elizabeth didn't know.

"Well, I think I saw him last night. At the football stadium. During the rally. And I was surprised to see he was still in town." Elizabeth faltered. She knew she was sounding incoherent, but she couldn't help it. "He said he was just staying until Tuesday."

"He changed his plans." Elsa definitely

sounded concerned now. "What exactly is the problem, Liz?"

Taking a deep breath, Elizabeth squared her shoulders again and said, "It's just that I noticed he looks—he looks just like—Donald Redman. The man the police are looking for."

There was a stunned silence. Elizabeth bit her lip, silently praying that her suspicions were wrong. She didn't want Elsa to be involved in any way.

Finally Elsa let out a shaky laugh. "You know, I told him the same thing," she confessed. "And I told him he should stay out of trouble while he's here, or else he'll regret it."

Elizabeth let her breath out in a rush. "Then you mean he's not—"

"He's an old friend from college, Liz. I've known him for years," Elsa assured her. "It's just a crazy coincidence, that's all. But I appreciate your calling me instead of going to the police," she added with another weak laugh.

"Sure." Elizabeth nodded automatically, her mind a whirl. It was just a coincidence. A case of mistaken identity, just as she thought it might be. She gulped. "No problem."

"Well, I really should get back to work."

"Sure. I'm really sorry. Honest."

"It's all right, Liz. Don't worry about it. Thanks for checking with me first."

As Elizabeth hung up the phone, she felt a mix of feelings: fear, doubt, relief, guilt, and humiliation. She believed Elsa, but the uncanny resemblance made her shudder. Flipping the picture facedown, she tried to put it out of her mind.

Elsa Bartel sat at her desk, her pulse pounding in her temples.

Did she believe me? I sounded so—so guilty.

Moaning, Elsa buried her face in her hands. It was all a nightmare. A nightmare she couldn't wake up from.

Donald! Why are you doing this to me?

Silently she cursed her brother for seeking her out. Twelve years ago, when Donald tried to kill their parents, he had been committed to the psychiatric hospital, and Elsa and her parents had left town. Mr. and Mrs. Redman were no longer living, and after Elsa's marriage, she and her husband had risked coming back to Sweet Valley.

But Donald had found her, and it was starting all over—the crazy, wild accusations, the sweet, reasonable apologies, the fear, the doubts, the nightmares.

She replayed the scene in her memory. She could almost hear Donald's voice in her ear.

"What was she doing here last night?" he had asked.

Elsa had stared at him. "Who?"

"*Her*. Melanie," Donald had said harshly. "Don't pretend you don't know."

Melanie was the name of the girl he had kidnapped, Elsa had remembered with a wave of shock. Melanie had been blond, pretty, cheerful. Just like Elizabeth.

"That was my baby-sitter, Donald," she had told him, eyes wide. "Melanie is a grown woman now."

Instantly the wild look had vanished from his eyes. "Of course, you're right," he had said sensibly. "My mistake."

Elsa had been satisfied at the time, but now . . . now she wasn't so sure he knew what reality was. Donald had always been crafty that way, reassuring her when inside he was still scheming. What if he really thought Elizabeth was Melanie? After all this time, he should have gotten over the rejection, but there was no way to know. His escape put her in an impossible position, and she couldn't decide what the best thing to do was.

I can't turn him in, though. He's still my brother. And he hasn't hurt anyone.

Yet. The word sent a chill of fear through her.

So far, Donald hadn't actually hurt anyone. But what would he do if he knew Elizabeth had seen through his disguise? she wondered. There was no telling how he would react, what he would plot. Especially if he was confusing her with Melanie. Especially if he still held a grudge.

Elsa's hands were damp from fear, and tears of confusion ran down her face. She felt completely helpless and alone. All she could do was pray Donald wasn't confusing Elizabeth with Melanie, pray he wasn't still looking for revenge.

What should I do? she asked herself. *What should I do?*

Thirteen

On Friday afternoon Jeffrey drove out to the mall. He wanted to buy himself some albums, along with a book of poems for Elizabeth.

An expectant smile on his face, Jeffery walked into Valley Sounds. But the day lost its sparkle when he spotted Bruce Patman at the cash register, laying down a credit card to buy a mountain of compact discs. Jeffrey turned his back and flipped blindly through a stack of albums while a wave of resentment washed over him. Coming home to find Bruce hanging all over Elizabeth had been a terrible shock. He couldn't understand why Elizabeth wouldn't even discuss the reasons for her friendship with Bruce.

"Well, well, well. If it isn't the fearless Ranger Jeff," came the lazy, insolent voice. "Shouldn't you be outside making a birchbark canoe or something?"

Jeffrey turned around slowly, keeping his temper under control. "That must be the funniest thing I've heard this year, Bruce."

"I thought you'd like it." Bruce grinned, and his dark eyes were taunting as he continued. "So, the weekend is here, huh? Yes, indeed. Friday night. Got a date, Ranger Jeff?"

"Yes." Jeffrey stared evenly at Bruce for a moment and then deliberately turned his back on him.

Bruce laughed, unaffected. He leaned back against the record bins and folded his arms across his chest. "Me, too," he said in a dreamy voice.

Ignoring him, Jeffrey kept his eyes fixed on the records in front of him. He wasn't about to take Bruce's bait and ask.

But Bruce didn't wait to be asked. He whistled softly through his teeth and said, "I, for one, will be seeing Liz tonight. How about you?"

"Get out of town," Jeffrey scoffed, his anger surging. He looked daggers at Bruce. "Liz and I are going to a movie tonight."

"Yeah?" Bruce gave him another cocky, challenging grin. "I'll bet you ten new albums you're wrong."

For a moment Jeffrey stared at Bruce with pure fury, his fist clenched as he contemplated punching Bruce right in the nose. But he took a deep breath and relaxed his hand. He wouldn't give Bruce the satisfaction of provoking a fight. Scowling, he pushed past Bruce to the exit.

"Forget it, Patman. You are really scum!"

Bruce's easy, mocking laughter followed Jeffrey out of the store. Livid, he stormed through the mall and out to his car.

What's going on, anyway? he asked himself in silent fury. *What is it with Liz and Bruce?*

Over and over, Elizabeth had told him to trust her, to take her word that there was nothing to worry about. But that wasn't enough, especially not with Bruce bragging about having a date with her. As he slammed his car door shut, Jeffrey resolved to find out once and for all.

I don't know what kind of game she's playing, but if she doesn't tell me tonight, she can forget it.

Elizabeth finished putting on her makeup—a faint sweep of color on her cheeks and a touch of pink lip gloss. She smiled at her reflection, then hurried downstairs. Jeffrey would arrive any minute to pick her up, and she wanted to be ready.

When she walked into the kitchen, she found Jessica and Lila debating the Endless Summer concert. She sat down with them and propped her elbows on the table.

"I think they'll cancel again," Lila declared in a know-it-all tone. "With Redman on the loose, they won't be taking any chances."

Jessica flared up. "No way! It's tomorrow night, and they aren't putting it off again. If they were, there would've been an announcement by now."

Thinking back to their "announcement" about the original delay, Elizabeth frowned. It had been a few days since she had consulted the Ouija board, and she wondered if she should try again. So far, it had been correct every time.

"Well, who knows?" Lila went on. She leaned back and shrugged. "If tomorrow night comes and that maniac blows up the stadium, we'll all be late starting school this year."

Jessica stared at her friend and giggled. "Gross, Lila."

"Lila's an optimist," Elizabeth put in with a lopsided grin. Usually her twin's best friend irritated her, but she was in too good a mood to let Lila bother her. Tonight would be her first real reunion with Jeffrey, and nothing could spoil it.

Elizabeth smiled and then looked up as the phone rang. "It's probably for you," she said to her sister. "It always is."

Jessica smirked and reached for the phone. "Hello?"

Elizabeth watched her, waiting. Her twin's expectant smile turned sour.

"For you," Jessica said, passing the receiver over her head with a grimace. *"Bruce."*

Elizabeth blushed. She avoided meeting Jessica's or Lila's eyes as she took the phone. "Hi, what's up?"

"Liz?" Bruce sounded tired and morose. "You aren't busy, are you?"

Elizabeth thought of Jeffrey, on his way to pick her up. Biting her lip, she said hesitantly, "Well, not right this minute."

"Oh—forget it. I'm interrupting—"

"No, don't worry about it," she cut in. "Really, it's not a problem. What's wrong?"

He sighed heavily. "I don't know. It's just getting me down so much. I was just in a tennis match on the school courts. And I got totally waxed, Liz. I can't do it anymore. I swear, it's no use."

Elizabeth felt a pang of sympathy. Tennis had always been Bruce's greatest talent. If he couldn't play anymore, it was probably a crushing disappointment.

"Bruce, maybe you're just in bad form today. Tomorrow you'll—"

"Tomorrow? Liz, don't you get it? I'm running out of tomorrows!" Bruce was beginning to sound desperate. "Why should I even keep trying? I don't know," he added with a wild laugh. "Why should I go on at all?"

"Wait!" Elizabeth's heart raced as she realized what he was saying. "Bruce, don't—whatever you're thinking, don't."

"That's easy for you to say," he replied bitterly. "I'm the one who's— Maybe I should just get it over with right now."

"No!" Elizabeth winced and cast an anxious glance at the clock. Then she made a decision. "Listen, just stay where you are. I'll meet you at the tennis courts. Just wait for me, OK?"

"Well . . . all right. I'll wait."

After slamming down the phone, Elizabeth grabbed the car keys from the kitchen counter and looked at the others. They were gazing at her with avid curiosity.

"Listen," she told them in a low, worried voice. "Jeffrey will be here any minute, but don't tell him where I went. Just say that I'll be back as soon as I can."

Jessica nodded, wide-eyed. "Sure, Liz."

Elizabeth turned and hurried out of the room. Jessica and Lila followed her to the front door.

"I guess you don't want Jeffrey to know you're meeting Bruce, right?" Jessica asked.

Rolling her eyes, Elizabeth said, "Right. It'll only make things worse. Just tell him there was an emergency, I'll be back as soon as I can, and not to worry about *anything.*" She looked hard at her twin. She wanted to make sure Jeffrey didn't get upset again or misconstrue the situation. "Will you tell him?"

"Sure," Jessica replied. She nudged Lila.

Lila nodded. "Sure."

"Thanks," Elizabeth said, relieved. She slung her bag over one shoulder and ran out the door. She had to get to Bruce before he did something drastic.

Lila's eyes narrowed as she watched Elizabeth drive away, and a sly, gleeful smile crossed her face. When Jeffrey arrived and found Elizabeth had left, he would be stunned. It would be the perfect opportunity for Lila to comfort him.

"Lila. Earth to Lila."

Glancing quickly at Jessica, Lila hoped her friend couldn't guess what she was thinking. "Sorry. I was spacing out."

"You're telling me."

Jessica turned and shut the door, then led the way to the back of the house. Lila followed a pace behind, thinking. The important thing was to get Jeffrey alone. She took a peek at her watch. It was quarter to eight. Elizabeth had said he was due any minute.

"I left something in my car," Lila said breathlessly, as though she had just remembered it. "Hang on, Jess. I'll be right back."

Before Jessica had a chance to say anything, Lila dashed out the front door. Once outside, she sat in her car, pretending to search for a lost item. She kept one eye out for Jeffrey's car while she rummaged around.

At last Lila saw Jeffrey's car round the corner. She waited a moment and then climbed out and casually slammed the door. She feigned surprise as Jeffrey pulled up at the curb behind her.

"Oh, hey, Jeffrey," she purred.

He strolled over to her, an easy smile on his face. "Hi, Lila. What's up?"

"Nothing much." She shrugged, then smiled flirtatiously. "Jess and I are just hanging out. Oh, I just—" She widened her eyes and clapped one hand over her mouth.

Jeffrey looked politely curious. "What?"

"I just remembered. You're here to pick up Liz, right?"

"Right." A tiny frown creased his forehead. "What about it?"

Wincing, Lila glanced over her shoulder at the house and dropped her voice. "Well, Liz just left, but she said she'd be right back. She didn't want you to worry."

Jeffrey leaned closer, intent and anxious. "What? Where did she go?"

An expression of regret on her face, Lila explained that Elizabeth had left right after Bruce called from the school tennis courts. "I—I think she's meeting him there," she said quietly. She made her voice sound disapproving and sad.

Jeffrey clenched his jaw tightly and looked off into the distance. His green eyes smoldered with anger.

"But she said she'd be back really soon," Lila rushed on. She looked at him in dismay. "You don't think . . ."

"I don't know what to think," he muttered. He looked down at her gravely. "Thanks for letting me know, Lila. I've got to get over to the courts."

With that he turned and strode back to his car, got in, and pulled away. The tires screeched as he turned the corner at the end of the street.

Lila nodded. She raised her eyebrows and rocked back and forth on her heels in satisfaction as she pictured the confrontation. "That's a scene I wish I could see," she murmured to herself.

Fourteen

Next, the red wire. Careful, gently. Take it easy—ah! Perfect.

Donald Redman picked up a tiny jeweler's screwdriver and delicately clamped the wire into place. His feverish eyes were fixed on his creation, his work of art, and a smile was frozen on his lips. The bomb was his own unique design. Once wired to strategically placed TNT and plastic, it could be activated by remote control from a safe distance. It would explode, setting off a chain reaction that would demolish the stadium and everyone in it.

Grimly efficient, Redman put the finishing touches on his masterpiece. Then he picked up the remote control. His eyes glowed with excitement, and a feeling of exhilaration coursed through him as his thumb edged toward the red button. He hit it. Instantly the digital clock began running backward from two minutes, and a red light on the detonator bomb began to pulsate.

Redman watched, fascinated, while the numbers flashed away in front of his eyes. Beads of sweat stood out on his forehead, and his breath came in short, sharp gasps. When the timer reached 1:05, he pressed his thumb on the button again. The clock froze, and the glowing red light went dark. Redman breathed a satisfied sigh.

"Perfect." The bomb was truly a masterpiece. It was almost too bad it would be blown to bits by its own power. But what a beautiful way to go!

He chuckled softly and sat back on his heels. A surveying glance around the utility room in the Sweet Valley High stadium told him he had everything he needed: coiled copper wire, cylinders of dynamite, the plastic explosive, which was the glue to hold it all in place, electrical tape, and his small kit of precision tools. It was almost time to start preparing the sticks that would blow the stadium into rubble. Nothing and no one could stop him now.

"The fools, they're so stupid," he said out loud. "All of them, so stupid."

He didn't even think the police were really

trying to find him. They were so stupid they didn't even suspect he might return to the scene of Wednesday night's little rehearsal. The Sweet Valley High stadium was deserted and empty. He had the run of the place. He could take his time, preparing everything for tomorrow night.

It was so simple to fool people, Redman thought. Even though the tennis courts next door were crowded, no one had noticed him. He was too smart. All he had had to do was act natural, look as though he had a legitimate reason for going into the stadium, and no one had given him a second glance.

Of course, there had been times in the last week that he had wanted to yell at people, "It's me! Donald Redman! You're so stupid, you can't even recognize me!" It was frustrating, in a way, not to be recognized for who he was—a unique, brilliant man.

All his life, people had either mocked or ignored him and had tried to take credit for the things he did. For as long as he could remember, everyone had cheated him, tried to ruin his chances. In the hospital it had been the same: robot nurses and smug, idiotic doctors who kept trying to "cure" him.

"But not anymore," he said with sudden rage. "Not this time."

He lunged to his feet and grabbed the dynamite, wire, plastic, and tape and yanked open the door to the corridor. His jaw was set, and a cold light blazed in his eyes. Breathing hard, he strode toward the nearest tunnel out to the stadium seats. He knew exactly where the TNT and plastic would go: one bundle each in sections A1, C3, D1, and F3. A ring of explosions all the way around the stadium. It would be utter devastation, chaos, carnage. They would be sorry they had ever made fun of Donald Redman.

The thought brought the happy smile back to his face, and he stepped with new energy into the passageway. Then he heard voices.

Redman flattened himself against the wall, all his senses alert and tuned for danger. Inch by inch, he crept forward until the voices became clearer.

"This is better," said a male voice. "The courts were so crowded. I just felt like I couldn't breathe."

"How about here?" The second speaker was a girl.

"Sure." There was a pause. Then, "I don't know. I don't know how much longer I can go on."

"You have to, Bruce. You can't give up. You still have a chance if you fight it."

Redman's heart raced with adrenaline. Fear

of discovery only added more excitement, more challenge to his mission. Confident that they wouldn't notice him, he edged toward the opening and risked a quick look. A boy and a girl, two teenagers, were sitting in the bleachers near the archway, their backs to him. Their heads were close together, and they were deep in conversation.

They won't notice me, Redman told himself gleefully. *I'm too smart for them*.

He watched them through narrowed eyes, waiting for them to leave so he could finish his job. The low murmur of their talk sounded faint to his ears as his pulse pounded in his temples. But he grew impatient as they kept talking. It didn't appear that they were planning to leave right away.

As though to confirm his suspicion, the girl reached for the boy's hand and shook her head vehemently. As she did Redman saw her face for the first time. A flash of anger ripped through him, nearly blinding him.

Melanie!

Redman backed up, his mind working frantically. What was Melanie doing there? What had she been doing at Elsa's house and at the stadium on Wednesday night?

Then he knew. She was *after* him. She was *following* him. She was trying to ruin everything. Then she would mock him and laugh at him when his plan failed.

Redman's face turned a blotchy red as he thought about Melanie. Somehow she knew. Why else would she have been at Elsa's, lying in wait for him with that absurd story about Elsa being out? A blatant liar, that's what she was. And now that he thought about it, hadn't she been at the movie theater on Monday, too? She had gone in with another girl, masquerading as a regular teenager. But he knew better now.

She was going to ruin everything, spoil his plans, just as she had done before. When he had tried to change her mind, tried to convince her of how brilliant he was, she had laughed at him and run away. She would do it again— unless he did something about it. Redman crept around the corner again and stared malevolently at her back.

You're not going to cheat me this time, he vowed silently. *This time I won't just steal you. This time I'll kill you.*

Shaking with relief because he had found out her plan in time, Redman tucked the dynamite more securely under his arm and headed back to the utility room to get ready.

Jessica flopped backward on her bed and reached for the volume knob on her stereo. She didn't know why, but she felt restless. She had a nagging feeling that something was wrong, but she didn't know what. She turned up the stereo, to block out her thoughts.

When Lila spoke to her, Jessica couldn't hear a thing she was saying. "What?" she asked the ceiling.

"I said, let's have another séance." Lila was turning the planchette around in her hands and humming.

Jessica sat up on one elbow. "I don't know. I'm not in the mood."

"Come on!" Lila persisted. "Just for fun."

Jessica's thoughts went back to the first few times they had duped Elizabeth. "We really did a number on Liz, didn't we?" she asked, chuckling.

Lila nodded. "We sure did. Come on, Jess. Just once more."

"Oh, all right." Jessica sat all the way up and crossed her legs while Lila spread the board between them on the bed. She half-closed her eyes and intoned, "Spirits from the 'other side'! Hear our prayers, we beseech you."

Lila let out a muffled giggle. "Jessica, you're such a ham."

"I know," Jessica agreed. "But so are you. Half the time we were fooling Liz, I was practically cracking up."

Their fingertips rested on the planchette, which they were taking turns moving. "OK, now. Get serious." She gave Lila a mock severe look and tried not to laugh.

Nodding solemnly, Lila lowered her eyes. The planchette swooped around the board, picking letters out of the alphabet. "Oh, boy. It's a hot one," Lila said lightly. "Not even waiting for a question."

"D-A-N-G-E-R," Jessica read. She looked up at Lila and smirked. "Cute. Nice dramatic touch there, Li."

Lila gave her a surprised grin. "Cute, yourself."

The planchette continued moving under their fingertips. Jessica waited to see what her friend was going to write.

"S-T-A-D-I-U-M. E-W," the board spelled.

"Danger, stadium, E.W." Jessica cocked her head to one side. "Funny, Lila."

Lila was watching the board, but she glanced up sharply as Jessica spoke. "I'm not doing anything."

"Give me a break!" Jessica scoffed. She knew she hadn't pushed the planchette, so Lila must have. A strange chill crept up her spine. "You were pushing, and I don't think it's very funny to say Liz is in danger at the stadium."

"But I didn't!" Lila was indignant, and her

voice shook slightly. "You were doing it," she repeated.

"I was not!"

"Stop it!" Jessica jerked her hands back. "Stop it! If that's your idea of a joke, it's horrible, Lila!" she cried out. Tears pricked her eyelids, and she jumped up off the bed, staring angrily at her friend and breathing hard.

Lila was shaking her head, staring wide-eyed back at Jessica. "I swear—"

"You were doing it!" Jessica insisted. Her heart was beating wildly. She didn't want to hear Lila keep protesting.

Her lower lip trembling, Lila repeated, "I swear, Jessica. I wasn't doing it." Lila stared at her friend. "Do *you* swear you weren't doing it?"

"Yes!" Outraged and frightened, Jessica picked up the planchette and hurled it across the room. It bounced off the wall and fell to the floor.

An ominous silence filled the bedroom. Neither one of them wanted to say what they were thinking, that the deadly serious message might be accurate.

Finally Lila whispered, "Do you think it's real?"

"No! Yes—I don't know!" Jessica gasped. "When you and I first started fooling around with the board, Liz told me that she heard that sometimes people subconsciously control the planchette, that thoughts in their subconscious come out, even though they don't realize it.'' Her mind was reeling.

"But why would you or I think something like that?'' Lila asked.

"Because Liz and I have always had this thing about knowing when the other is in trouble. A lot of identical twins have it.''

"What are we going to do?''

"I don't *know*!'' Jessica pressed one hand against her mouth. She had never been more frightened and confused in her whole life.

"Do you think Liz—''

"She's not at the stadium, anyway,'' Jessica broke in, her voice trembling. She's at the tennis courts with Bruce.'' She didn't want to think about the fact that the courts were next to the stadium, that the empty stadium was a good place for a private conversation—especially in Bruce's opinion.

Lila wet her lips nervously. "But what kind of trouble could she be in at the stadium? I mean, she went to meet Bruce, and even if they're sitting at the stadium, it's not like he would hurt Liz. I mean, he's not the Mad Bomber, or anything.''

Horrified, Jessica stared at Lila. "Redman," she whispered.

"We'll call the police," Lila decided. She grabbed the telephone. "We'll tell them—"

"Tell them the Ouija board told us my sister is in danger at the stadium and that we *think* Redman might be there? They'll think we're crazy."

"Well—well—" Lila didn't know what to say; she knew Jessica was right.

Jessica paced back and forth, trying to concentrate. *Think,* she ordered herself sternly. *Think.*

Suddenly she knew what they had to do. "Come on," she said fiercely, racing for the door.

Lila stumbled after her. "What?"

"We have to go to the stadium! We have to save Liz!"

Fifteen

Jessica galloped down the stairs nearly tripping, and Lila raced after her. Frantic and close to tears, Jessica wished desperately that her parents were home. She didn't know if she and Lila could handle this by themselves. But Mr. and Mrs. Wakefield were out at a cocktail party and wouldn't be home for hours. Jessica stopped in the hallway, paralyzed by indecision.

"Liz took the car," she realized, stunned. "How are we going to—"

Lila grabbed her wrist. "My car," she pointed out sensibly. "Come on."

Just as Jessica reached for the doorknob, she heard running footsteps outside, followed by impatient knocking. "Oh, no," she groaned, opening the door, ready to brush past whomever it was without stopping.

"Liz! You're home! I have to talk to—"

"I'm sorry," Jessica blurted out, interrupting the blond woman on the doorstep and running past her. "I have to go. My sister's in trouble."

"What did you say?"

The horror and pain in the woman's voice broke through Jessica's blind flight. She turned and stared. "Liz is in danger," she whispered. "I don't know why, but I-I have this feeling it may have something to do with that psycho Redman."

"Oh, no!" the woman whispered. "I was afraid this would happen."

Jessica and Lila exchanged a startled look.

"I'm Elsa Bartel. Liz baby-sits for my son sometimes," the woman continued. She ran one hand through her hair distractedly. "Donald— Donald came to my house one night, and Liz recognized him. He'll do more than just hurt her if he's got her now," she said, shuddering. "He's mixing her up with someone he used to know, a girl named Melanie. I thought—I hoped —he had left town after that phony bomb scare at the stadium. But he came to my house this afternoon, asking me where Melanie was—where I was hiding her. I knew that he meant Liz. I came to tell her—"

Jessica felt a mixture of confusion, fear, and impatience. "What do you mean? Donald?"

Elsa raised a ravaged face and looked Jessica in the eye. "He's my brother. I should have gone to the police right away, but he's my only living relative, and I couldn't." Her voice broke. "Then when he showed up this afternoon looking for this girl he thinks is Melanie, he kept mumbling about showing all those jocks that he was smarter than they were. He was incoherent, but he said something about the stadium." She began sobbing. "I decided I'd come over here and warn Liz and then report my brother to the police."

Mrs. Bartel made an effort to pull herself together. "Where's Liz now?"

Tears rolled down Jessica's cheeks. "The stadium," she said. "Liz met someone at the tennis courts at school, but I'm pretty sure she's at the stadium."

Mrs. Bartel said firmly, "Then we have to call the police right now. There's a concert at the stadium tomorrow night, right?" Jessica nodded, and Elsa continued. "He always swore he would get revenge. I thought the fake bomb might be it. But after today. . . ." Her voice shook as she said, "If Liz walks in on him, or he spots her, she's in terrible danger. He has a persecution complex. He always thinks people are trying to hurt him."

Jessica and Lila looked at each other. So far,

Elsa hadn't asked how *they* knew Elizabeth was in danger. But it didn't matter now. "You can use our phone. Come inside," Jessica said.

"I'll tell them what I know, what I suspect," Mrs. Bartel said as they hurried through the house to the phone in the kitchen. "They have to meet us at the stadium. They have to. I'll never forgive myself if anything happens to Liz."

The sudden tone of authority in the woman's voice reassured Jessica. "Liz is with a boy we know, too," she added. "Bruce Patman."

Beside her, Lila swallowed audibly. "And probably Jeffrey."

"What?" Jessica gasped while Elsa dialed the police. Surprised, Jessica looked at her friend. "How did he . . . ?"

"I told him," Lila whispered. Her face was white.

There was no time to delve any deeper. Jessica shook her head and tried to focus on the immediate crisis.

"Yes, that's right," Mrs. Bartel said after a terse but emotional explanation to the police. "But there may be at least another teenager out there, too. No, I'm not sure, but—right. Yes, Officer. I will. I can get there in ten minutes."

"OK?" Jessica asked nervously when Elsa hung up the phone.

167

"Come on. Let's go."

Without further delay, the three ran out of the house and headed for the football stadium.

"I just keep thinking about what happens when you—after you—" Bruce choked up and looked down at his hands, clenching and twisting them together. His lips trembled.

Elizabeth watched him helplessly, her heart aching. She wished there was something she could do to take away his sadness.

He raised dark, luminous eyes to her face. "Liz, I'm so afraid."

"Oh, Bruce!" Impulsively Elizabeth put her arms around him, and Bruce hugged her back hard. "I know," she whispered, filled with compassion and tenderness. "I know."

"Liz, Liz," he murmured.

With her eyes closed, Elizabeth sat holding Bruce in a tight embrace. His cheek was pressed against her neck, and for a moment she thought she felt him kiss the curve of her shoulder. Then she realized Bruce's lips moved because he was fighting tears. Ashamed of thinking he would take advantage of the situation, she held him even tighter.

"Oh, Bruce," she sighed, almost crying.

Bruce lifted his head so that his face was just

inches from Elizabeth's and stared deep into her eyes. Elizabeth felt a bond being forged between them, felt as though she were seeing right into his soul.

"Liz," he whispered, his voice hoarse.

She stared back at him. She was speechless with emotion.

"What the—" Jeffrey's shocked voice cut through the silence.

Elizabeth whirled around and fixed indignant eyes on her boyfriend, who was standing at the bottom of the bleachers and glaring up at them. All she could think of was that he had deliberately ignored her request to wait for her at home and that he had shattered a special, deeply personal moment between her and Bruce.

"What are you doing?" she demanded, suddenly furious with him.

"What am *I* doing?" Jeffrey's voice was incredulous. Taking the steps two at a time, he strode up to their seat. "What exactly are *you and Bruce* doing?" he asked in a bitterly sarcastic tone.

Bruce looked heavenward and let out a silent whistle. He didn't comment.

"I asked you to wait," Elizabeth said, standing up. "I would have been home in a few minutes. Can't you trust me at all?"

"It doesn't look like it."

169

With a gasp of indignation, Elizabeth looked at Bruce, then at Jeffrey again. "You really think—when I *told* you—" Anger made her stumble over her words.

"No, you didn't tell me," Jeffrey stormed on. "You won't tell me what is so fascinating about Bruce that you keep sneaking off with him behind my back."

"*Sneaking!*" Elizabeth choked out. She put her hands on her hips and tried to control her mounting anger and disappointment. She couldn't believe Jeffrey could act so immature. "It's *supposed* to be a secret," she told him furiously, flashing a look at Bruce.

Bruce looked away, not saying anything. He was beginning to look as though he wished he were somewhere else.

But Jeffrey laughed scornfully. "A secret? Some secret, when Mr. Irresistible here was bragging he had a date with you tonight."

"Right, Jeffrey," Elizabeth sneered. "Exactly how was he supposed to know—" She faltered to a stop as Jeffrey's words finally caught up with her.

Puzzled, she looked at Bruce. He was sitting with his elbows on the seat behind them, looking innocently off into the distance. The glimmer of sunset lit his face with a warm, vital glow. He had never looked more alive, healthy, and attractive. As Elizabeth frowned at him, confused, he turned his head and gave her a sheepish grin.

A sick feeling washed over Elizabeth, but she still didn't want to put her suspicion into words. Forcing herself, she asked, "Bruce, are you or are you not sick?"

"*Sick?*" Jeffrey sounded surprised.

Bruce looked thoughtful. "Well, not—exactly *sick*, but I think I'm about to get a major headache."

"Oh, no!" In an instant all the pieces of the puzzle fell into place. Elizabeth sat down hard on the seat. A dull flush of humiliation spread across her face.

It had been a hoax, right from the beginning. Suddenly Elizabeth didn't know how she could have been so gullible. Somehow Jessica and Lila had pushed all the right buttons, and she had believed everything the Ouija board said. Elizabeth felt sick to her stomach.

"Liz?" Jeffrey was looking at her, a worried expression on his face.

Tears of embarrassment and anger built up behind Elizabeth's lashes and spilled over. Nearly blinded, she stood up and pushed past Jeffrey. She had to be alone.

"Liz! Wait!"

Ignoring Jeffrey's call, she headed for the tunnel leading out of the stadium. She wanted to be by herself, to crawl into a secluded hole. Jessica and Lila had made a complete fool of her with the Ouija board, and she cringed when she remembered all the things she had said and done. It was awful. And Bruce had been in on it, too. When she thought of the starry-eyed way she had taken him in her arms, she thought she would die of mortification.

"How could I be so stupid?" Elizabeth wailed out loud. "How could I be so *dumb*?"

Up ahead, she saw the door marked Utility Room. She decided to hide there in case Jeffrey came looking for her. She couldn't face anyone right now, especially not Jeffrey. Stifling her sobs, she reached the utility room and yanked open the door.

What she saw made her stop in her tracks. Even to an inexperienced person, it was obvious the room had been converted into a make-shift bomb factory. It didn't take a bomb expert to read the letters *TNT* on the case in the middle of the room. But even as she stepped back to run for help, the door slammed behind her.

She turned and her heart skipped a beat.

"Redman!"

"Hello, Melanie."

Sixteen

Elizabeth managed one terrified scream for help before Redman grabbed her.

"Shut up!" he hissed, twisting her arm up behind her back.

With a stifled yelp, Elizabeth bit her lip to keep from crying out. Daggers of pain ripped up her arm, but she hardly noticed. Her eyes were glued to what was obviously a bomb on a folding chair in the corner. She knew now that Elsa had lied to her, but she didn't understand why. All she understood was that she was in the power of a dangerous, escaped psychopath. Her fear was so intense she could hardly stand.

"This is the last time," Redman added. His breath was hot on her neck. "You thought you could trick me again, Melanie, but I'm too smart for you."

Elizabeth's frozen mind couldn't grasp the

meaning of his words. It didn't make any sense. Trick him? What was he talking about? And why was he calling her Melanie?

Keeping her arm forced up behind her, Redman edged around to the door and opened it a crack. He gave her a sly, calculating smile. His normally attractive face was now tight and distorted with madness. His blue eyes glittered almost sightlessly, as though focused on some bizarre inner vision.

"Scream again."

She stared at him. "What?"

"Scream *again*, Melanie."

When she still couldn't make herself do what he said, Redman gave her arm a fierce wrench. A scream of pain tore out of Elizabeth's throat, and her eyesight grew blurry for a moment. While she staggered dizzily, Redman pulled her away from the door and waited.

They heard running footsteps, two pairs.

"Liz? Where are you?"

"This way! She's down here somewhere!"

Two voices: Jeffrey's and Bruce's. Weak with fear, Elizabeth moaned, "No!" before Redman hissed at her to be silent. His grip on her arms was strong and unrelenting.

The footsteps slowed. Elizabeth counted her heartbeats as the two boys came closer. There was nothing she could do to keep them from falling into Redman's trap. Half of her wanted them to rescue her, and the other half begged them to run for help. Trembling, she closed her eyes.

Redman deliberately nudged the door. It closed with a definite click.

"In here! Liz?"

The door burst open, and Jeffrey and Bruce rushed inside. They both stopped dead when they saw Elizabeth and Redman. Jeffrey took an involuntary step forward, but he froze as Redman twisted Elizabeth's arm again. Jeffrey's face went white at Elizabeth's muffled sob.

"Don't move," Redman ordered.

Elizabeth met Jeffrey's eyes mutely. It was too late to tell him how sorry she was.

Redman jerked his head toward the back of the room. "OK, over there. Go on."

Warily the two boys moved around the bomb, the TNT, the tools and coils of wire, never taking their eyes off Redman and Elizabeth. When they reached the back wall, Redman kicked the door shut again.

"OK, now we're all here," he said in a smug, satisfied voice. He chuckled. Then, without warning, he shoved Elizabeth away from him.

She stumbled across the small, crowded room, and Jeffrey and Bruce both jumped forward to catch her.

"Get back!"

The three teenagers straightened, staring in helpless anger at Redman. He was holding a small device in his hand, a flat black box with a switch on it. Elizabeth felt a shiver of dread run through her.

"Now, just so you know," Redman said quietly, "this remote control will trigger the bomb." He pointed to the construction of dynamite, wires, and dials on the chair. "So I'd like you all to keep as quiet as little mice while I finish up what I have to do. If you try anything, I hit the switch."

Elizabeth shrank backward against the wall. Jeffrey put one arm around her in a protective gesture. Their eyes met briefly, but they didn't speak. Next to them, Bruce was standing with his arms crossed in his usual arrogant posture, but his face was pale.

Redman gave them an ominous look, then began bundling together sticks of dynamite. He wrapped them with electrical tape, all the while muttering under his breath. Aside from his angry whisperings, the room was deadly quiet.

After a few moments of grim silence, Bruce cleared his throat. "You hit that switch and you go, too."

Redman leapt to his feet. "You think I'm a fool, don't you!" The sudden mad fury in his voice shocked them all. He glared at them wildly. "You really think I would make a bomb that can kill me? I'm the *only* one this bomb *can't* kill!"

"How does it work?" Bruce asked in a calm voice. Elizabeth realized Bruce was trying to stall for time. At the same moment Jeffrey squeezed her shoulder, as though trying to communicate.

"Yeah," Elizabeth rasped. She licked her lips and forced a polite smile. "It sounds incredible."

Redman narrowed his eyes suspiciously. For a second Elizabeth was afraid he saw through their ploy. But then he relaxed and actually chuckled.

"Well, it is incredible, I know," he admitted. His tone was boastful. "It's about the most sophisticated thing I ever designed. It's one of a kind—a real masterpiece."

"Can it blow up the whole stadium?" asked Jeffrey. His voice had a tight sound to it.

"Not exactly." Redman pursed his lips thoughtfully. "See, I'm hooking it up to these bundles of dynamite. I'll connect them all with this wire here, and when I hit the remote, this baby's gonna blow and set off the others." He gave the bomb a gentle, almost loving pat and smiled to himself.

Elizabeth also smiled, but inside, she was

quaking with fear. Redman was completely insane, but he was smart enough to construct a devastating bomb, crazy enough to use it, and crazy enough to believe it actually couldn't hurt him.

Before she realized what she was saying, Elizabeth whispered, "Why?"

"Why?" Redman turned to her, his good humor evaporating. He took two steps. "You! You always laugh at me! You think you're so clever. You really thought you could trick me again, Melanie. Me!"

Confused and frightened, Elizabeth shook her head. "I don't know what—"

"Shut up!"

Jeffrey's arm tightened around Elizabeth. She pressed against him to keep from shaking, but her knees felt weak. That was the second time Redman had called her Melanie and accused her of trying to trick him. She didn't know why he was so suspicious of her. Was it because she had recognized him at the school spirit rally? But she hadn't made the connection then. Or had she? She couldn't remember.

Then it hit her. The girl Redman had kidnapped. Did he think she was— Elizabeth shook her head. She didn't know what to think.

"She thought I was dumb enough to fall into her trap," Redman muttered to himself. He stalked back to the bundles of dynamite and began fitting lengths of wire to them. In spite of his preoccupied ramblings, however, the remote control was never more than inches from his hand.

"Me! Dumb! Everyone always underestimates me. And they're doing it again. The fools! Idiots! You thought you could make fun of me, you dumb jocks."

Elizabeth listened with horrified fascination to the man's ravings. "I'm a genius, a giant among men. But I've been persecuted and hounded, betrayed by enemies on every side. But I'll show you all. I'm going to destroy your precious football stadium. I planned on doing it tomorrow night but now that you're here I'll have to blow it up tonight."

Elizabeth shook her head, silently saying, *No! No, don't do it!*

Redman cut off a piece of wire with a savage clip of his shears. "Everyone will be sorry now," he growled.

He spun around, glaring at them with narrowed eyes. "What are you doing?"

Jeffrey gaped at him. "Nothing."

"Yes, you are! All of you! You're trying to trick me again!"

"No!" Elizabeth held out one hand. "Please! We're not doing anything! We're not who you think we are."

Sneering, Redman shook his head and tossed

the remote control from one hand to the other. Elizabeth watched it, hardly breathing. "You think you're so smart," he muttered. "You think I don't know who you really are? All of you? You'll never leave here alive. That's how *smart* you are," he said viciously.

He grinned and held out the remote control in the palm of his hand. With his eyes on Elizabeth, he moved his thumb to the switch.

"It won't hurt me," he went on. "When I hit this switch, it'll be over for you and your cute boyfriends, Melanie. But I'll walk out of here a free man."

"I'm—not—Melanie," Elizabeth insisted.

"Sure." Redman chuckled. "Nice try."

Numb, Elizabeth stared at the switch. There was nothing they could do. There was no way out. As she shook her head in mute terror, Redman's maniacal laughter filled the room and echoed in her ears.

Jessica leapt out of the car the moment it stopped and dashed toward the stadium entrance.

"No! Jessica, stop!"

Even though Mrs. Bartel's words reached her, Jessica took several more steps before she halted. She felt an almost magnetic pull dragging her inside.

Mrs. Bartel pointed to a blue Toyota. "That's the car Donald was driving when he came to my house this afternoon. I have no idea how he got it, but I know that's the car he was driving. If Liz is really here, you'll only make things worse!"

Tears of frustration welled up in Jessica's eyes. She had to do something. Turning to Mrs. Bartel she said, "Just to be sure, I'm going to check the tennis courts." She could see the Fiat she and Elizabeth shared parked near the courts, as well as Bruce's Porsche.

"I'll go with you," Lila said.

"Be careful," Mrs. Bartel warned.

"We will," Jessica called, already racing off in the direction of the courts. Jessica and Lila quickly scanned the group standing around the courts. As Jessica had feared, there was no sign of Elizabeth, Bruce—or Jeffrey, either.

Lila grabbed Jessica's arm. "Tom McKay's over there," she said. "Let's ask him if he's seen them."

Tom was talking to some other members of the tennis team as the two girls approached. "Tom," Jessica called anxiously, "have you seen my sister or Bruce?"

Tom looked around. "They were here a little while ago, but I think they headed off toward the stadium."

It took all Jessica's self-control to keep from bursting into tears. "Thanks, Tom," she said, turning quickly and walking away. Lila followed her.

Mrs. Bartel was anxiously watching the two girls as they walked toward her. "They're inside," Jessica said tersely.

Mrs. Bartel reached out and put a comforting hand on Jessica's arm. "I know how hard this is, but we have to wait for the police. We *have* to."

Nodding, Jessica looked down at the ground. She had never been good at waiting, and now it was the only thing she could do that might save her twin's life.

A grim silence enveloped them, but they exchanged a look of relief when they heard the wail of a police siren. They watched in silence while a patrol car pulled into the parking lot and stopped next to them. Two officers jumped out and hurried toward Elsa Bartel.

"Are you Mrs. Bartel? What exactly is going on here?" one of them asked. "Donald Redman is your brother?"

In a faint, shaky voice, Elsa repeated her story. She pointed out her brother's car and told the police that she had a very good reason to believe her brother was planning to blow up the stadium and that it was possible he had three teenagers with him.

"Did he tell you all this?" The second officer stared at her in disbelief.

"Not exactly. But I know him better than anyone else does. Not that I understand him," Elsa went on. "But it all makes sense. He has bitter memories associated with the school and the football stadium, and you know that he's already planted a fake bomb here."

The first officer nodded and hurried back to the squad car to radio the police station.

"We'll have to set up some kind of communication link," the other one said brusquely. "We have to figure out just what we're dealing with."

"I'll talk to him. It might help." Elsa kept her voice firm, but her expression was filled with grief.

Finally Jessica burst out, "My sister is in the stadium, too. He may be holding her hostage. And two boys."

"Friends of ours," Lila added in a whisper.

Tears spilled down Jessica's cheeks again as the two police officers talked in the patrol car. She couldn't believe what was happening. It was a nightmare. Her sister was inside with a lunatic who might kill her.

And it's all my fault. Why did we have to pull that stupid trick on her? She wouldn't even be here if she didn't think Bruce was dying!

Through a blur of tears, Jessica watched patrol car after patrol car pull into the stadium parking lot. A police van also raced up, and Jessica felt her knees go weak when she saw the black-garbed SWAT team file out. They carried rifles and protective bomb gear.

"Where's the sister?" the leader of the SWAT team called out.

Instantly the crowd of police was conferring with Elsa. With a silent nod, she took a megaphone that was handed to her and continued to listen. Short, sharp orders flew at the crowd, and police ran to cover all the stadium exits.

"Is there a way for him to talk to us?" somebody yelled above the noise.

"We'll get some men inside the corridor with parabolic microphones. If a mouse sneezes, we'll hear it," another man said.

Lila held Jessica's hand in a tight grip. Jessica turned to her friend with silent grief. There was nothing they could do but wait.

Seventeen

Elizabeth was shaking. She tried to make herself stop by thinking about other things, but Redman's threats and psychopathic ramblings made it impossible. The small, cramped room was a prison.

"You'll be sorry," Redman said again. It was a theme he came back to over and over. "They'll all be sorry when I get through."

Scowling, he twisted two ends of wire together with his pliers. No matter how violent and irrational his words, his hands moved with steady precision. Already he had a stack of dynamite bundles that, according to him, could blow up the entire stadium and half the surrounding parking lot. Now all he needed to do was plant them and connect them to the main bomb sitting in the middle of the room.

Jeffrey, I love you, Elizabeth said silently.

With all her heart she wished there were a way for her to communicate with her boyfriend, to share the last few minutes with him. But she didn't dare speak. Every time she opened her mouth Redman seemed to redouble his fury.

Instead, she held Jeffrey's hand, thankful that at least they were together. In a strange way the danger that confronted Elizabeth made everything else easier to bear. Just minutes earlier she had been furious with her sister and Lila, had felt humiliated by Bruce and, most of all, disgusted with herself. Now none of it mattered. More than anything in the world she wished she could be with Jessica.

"Redman!" A voice boomed through the corridor. "This is the police!"

With a gasp of shock, Redman flattened himself against the wall next to the door. His face was twisted in outrage, and he gripped the remote control in his fist.

Elizabeth felt a surge of hope and relief in her heart, then a new wave of fear. Redman was already desperate. A police stampede would surely tip the scales. Sending a frightened look at Jeffrey, she pressed herself into the corner, as far from the bomb as possible. She gripped Jeffrey's hand with both of hers.

"This is the police. The stadium is surrounded."

"Come out with my hands up?" Redman second-guessed sarcastically. He let out a wild cackle. "Never." He opened the door a crack and shouted, "Never! Do you hear me? Never!"

"Come on, Redman. Be reasonable!"

Redman whirled around and glared at Elizabeth. "You did this!" he screamed. "You did this to me!"

Stunned, Elizabeth cried out, "No, I swear I didn't. I never—" Her throat closed up as Redman looked at the remote control in his hand. "No! Don't!" she croaked. She held out both hands, saw them shake. "Please!"

"Why shouldn't I?" he shot back. "You deserve it. All of you!"

"Donald? Donald, can you hear me?"

The color drained from Redman's face. Narrowing his eyes suspiciously, he moved back to the door, listening.

"Donald? It's me—Elsa. Your sister."

Elsa Bartel. Elizabeth had gone too far into shock to be surprised. She just prayed there was something the woman could do.

"You're lying!" Redman shouted out into the corridor. "You're not my sister!"

"Donald, you know it's me! Remember—" There was a pause, then Elsa's voice could be heard again. "Remember how you taught me about astronomy? How to find the Big Dipper and Orion and the North Star? We'd sit in the backyard, and you would show me all the constellations—"

As Redman listened to Elsa's voice, his jaw trembled. Something she said must have triggered a buried memory because unexpectedly he started to cry.

"Why are they doing this to me?" he demanded, to himself more than to anyone in particular. "Why do they always try to trick me?"

"Can I come in and talk to you? I want to talk to you, Donald!"

He took a quick look out the door and ducked back in again. The hand with the remote control was down at his side, and all his attention seemed to be fixed on his sister. Tears ran down his face.

"Is Elizabeth with you?"

Redman threw a distraught look back at the three in the corner. Elizabeth nodded once, her eyes wide.

"You're Melanie," he whimpered. He seemed to see her for the first time. "Melanie?"

Elizabeth gulped. "No. My name is Elizabeth."

"Let her go, Donald. And anyone else with you. We can talk about it. Come out, please!"

"No—no!" Trembling and confused, Redman shook his head. He didn't seem to be aware of Elizabeth and the boys anymore. "It's not really Elsa," he muttered. "It's just someone who sounds like her."

Suddenly Elizabeth became aware of the tension in Jeffrey's muscles. Almost imperceptibly he inched away from the wall, his gaze locked on the remote control in Redman's hand.

Elizabeth was paralyzed. She lifted her eyes to Jeffrey's face but couldn't speak. Her heartbeat was thundering in her ears. Jeffrey drew a deep breath and then hurled himself across the room, taking Redman down in a flying tackle.

Redman screamed like an animal, and the remote control flew out of his grasp. It bounced off the wall and skittered out of sight under a large cabinet. On the floor, Jeffrey was wrestling with Redman, who fought back with insane frenzy. Bruce threw himself down to help Jeffrey subdue the madman.

"Too late!" Redman gasped. "I hit it!"

189

"Liz! Bruce! Get out of here!" Jeffrey struggled for breath.

Before Elizabeth could move, Bruce pushed himself up, grabbed the bomb, and headed for the door.

"BRUCE! NO!" Her scream echoed out into the corridor.

Bruce was gone.

As though electrified, Elizabeth tore across the room and began scrabbling under the cabinet. The remote control was just beyond reach. She had to get it and stop it before it triggered the bomb.

"Jeffrey! Help me!"

As soon as Jeffrey realized what Elizabeth was trying to do, he jumped off Redman and hurried to her side. Redman scrambled to his feet and ran out after Bruce.

"Give it back!" Redman yelled. His voice echoed down the corridor. "Give it baaaaack!"

"I can't reach it!" Elizabeth gasped. Her arm was stretched as far as it could go under the cabinet, but it wasn't far enough. "Help me! Push!"

Without a word, Jeffrey put his shoulder to the heavy cabinet and strained to move it. A scraping noise accompanied the cabinet's fraction-of-an-inch shift. Elizabeth quickly changed her position to the side of the cabinet and reached from the back. Her muscles and tendons ached from the effort, but her fingertips finally brushed the small black box. Redman's description of his powerful bomb kept screaming in her mind, and Bruce had run off with it in his hands. She had to get the remote control!

"More! Oh, God!" she cried as tears of desperation streamed down her face.

Jeffrey's face was red with exertion, and his feet slipped on the smooth cement floor as he kept pushing. The cabinet gave another piercing screech, and this time Elizabeth got two fingers on the smooth, flat box.

"I—almost—" She pulled the box up against the wall, trying to get a better grip. "Oh, no," she groaned in agony as it slipped out of her grasp and clattered to the floor again.

Jeffrey heaved once more, and Elizabeth jammed her shoulder into the space. Her fingers trembled so much she could hardly lift it, but she snatched up the remote control and yanked it out. The digital numbers were rippling away, with only seconds left.

"What do I do? What should I do?"

"Smash it—rip out the wires!" Jeffrey yelled.

Praying feverishly, Elizabeth picked up the remote and smashed it down on the corner of a filing cabinet. The plastic casing splintered in her hands, cutting her. But she ignored the pain and plucked desperately at the wires inside, yanking them out. The clock, still intact, suddenly stopped.

Elizabeth stared up at Jeffrey in disbelief. "We did it!" she breathed.

Then a deafening explosion knocked them both to the floor.

Eighteen

Jessica didn't scream when she heard the explosion. The police shouted and ran into the stadium, but for her, the world had come to a stop. She didn't know if she was breathing or if her heart was beating. All she could see was the trail of smoke rising from inside the stadium. She stood isolated in a sea of noise, wailing sirens, and jostling police. Spectators from the tennis courts were huddled around in frightened groups. An ambulance maneuvered into position, as close to the entrance as possible.

"Jessica! Jessica!" Lila was screaming at her, tugging on her arm.

Slowly Jessica focused her eyes on her friend. Lila's face was blotched with tears. Lila didn't seem real. Nothing seemed real.

"Jessica, don't look like that!"

"She's OK," Jessica whispered.

Lila shook her head, her eyes filled with doubt and pity. "You don't know that—"

"I'd know," she insisted in a fierce growl. She pulled her arm out of Lila's grasp and started moving away. "I'd know if—" Without finishing her sentence, she ran toward the stadium.

"You can't go in, miss." A fire fighter caught her and held her back.

"You don't understand!" she shrieked. She struggled wildly in his arms. "I have to!"

He shook his head. "I'm sorry. We can't let you."

Suddenly weak, Jessica sagged and would have fallen if he hadn't caught her. Violent tremors shook her body as she leaned against a squad car. Someone put a comforting arm around her, but she wasn't even aware of who it was. It was as though she wouldn't come alive again until she saw her sister.

Liz, come out. Come out, darn it! You have to come out!

Stunned, Elizabeth pushed herself up to her knees. Her ears were ringing, and she could see smoke and dust billowing down the corridor past the door. For a moment her mind was a complete blank. She couldn't take in what had

194

happened. Beside her, Jeffrey was holding himself up against the cabinet, shaking his head. She reached out for him instinctively.

Then—*Bruce!*

It didn't matter anymore what Bruce had done or said in the past. He had taken the bomb, and the bomb had exploded. Fresh tears ran down her cheeks as she staggered to her feet and headed for the door, crying his name.

"Liz—no!" Jeffrey heaved himself up and caught her wrist. His eyes were bleak. "Don't."

Sobbing, Elizabeth yanked her arm away. "I have to. Bruce could still be—"

Jeffrey took her in his arms and held her tight as she cried, from shock, grief, and fear. And he was crying, too.

"No one could have made it through that blast, Liz," he choked. "It's no use."

"We have to see," Elizabeth said through bitter tears. "If there's any chance . . ."

She couldn't bring herself to utter the words. Lifting her eyes to Jeffrey's face, she said, "Please."

Nodding, Jeffrey took her hand. Together they walked out into the corridor. Smoke drifted past them, and a glow of flames flickered farther down, around the bend. They choked and coughed with every step, and their eyes stung with tears.

Elizabeth paused, fighting for air, and squinted into the dim, hazy light. Suddenly she saw a shadowy figure limping toward them. She stiffened. "Redman," she gasped, once again panicked.

"What?" Jeffrey started forward and stopped. "It's— I don't believe it!" He started running.

Elizabeth stared.

"Bruce!" she screamed, joy and relief sweeping through her. She ran, and with Jeffrey she grabbed Bruce as he stumbled and fell against the wall.

His hair was singed, his cheek was bleeding from two deep scratches, and his face was streaked with soot. But he was alive! He sank to his knees, gagging and coughing, but he managed a weak smile as he looked up at Elizabeth. The whites of his eyes showed bright in his blackened face.

"Hi, Goldilocks," he whispered faintly.

"Bruce! You're alive! You're alive!" Elizabeth was crying and laughing at the same time as she hugged him. "What happened?"

Running footsteps pounded in the corridor behind them. A swarm of police, guns drawn, and fire fighters raced in their direction. "Don't move!"

The three teenagers tensed at the sight of the

guns. Jeffrey waved both hands through the smoke. "It's us—Redman got away."

Bruce made a strangled sound in his throat and shook his head. He winced with pain, and Elizabeth's heart lurched in sympathy.

"What happened, son?" One of the police officers knelt down next to Bruce. "Are you OK? Where's Redman? Where did he go?"

Speechless, Bruce waved his hand back toward the center of the blast. Then he shook his head again.

A chill went through Elizabeth. She watched silently as half a dozen armed police ran down the corridor into the smoke. She turned questioning eyes to Bruce, and Jeffrey took her hand, squeezing hard. The remaining police officers huddled around to listen.

"He grabbed it from me and ran," Bruce whispered, his voice hoarse. He swallowed with difficulty and put one hand over his eyes. "He was—he was laughing—" The memory overwhelmed him, and he lowered his head.

Feeling sick, Elizabeth put her arms around Bruce. The horror was too great to think about. Bruce had just barely escaped with his life, but Redman had died a grisly death at his own hands.

"Come on," Jeffrey said in a gentle voice. "You're bleeding. You need a doctor."

At that moment one of the police officers returned through the smoke. His face was grim and pale. When he joined the other officers, he shook his head. The fire fighters headed through the smoke with extinguishers ready.

"Seal off the area," the leader ordered briskly. Police ran ahead to relay what had happened. Turning to Elizabeth, Jeffrey, and Bruce, the officer added, "Let's get you kids outside. When you're ready, you can tell us what happened."

As Elizabeth and Jeffrey helped Bruce to his feet, they exchanged a wordless look. Bruce had risked his life to save theirs, but Elizabeth didn't know how to express her gratitude.

"Thanks," Jeffrey said simply, gripping Bruce's shoulder. His voice cracked with emotion. "You—"

They were silent, but they all knew they were thinking the same thing. Together they had gone through a nightmare in the stadium, and somehow they had survived. It wasn't something they could talk about, and Elizabeth knew they would never be able to describe what had *really* happened to them, deep inside. The horrific experience had left an indelible mark on their souls.

Together they turned and slowly walked away.

A SWAT team member ran out of the front entrance and spoke briefly to the crowd of officers around Elsa Bartel. Through a haze, Jessica saw him shake his head, and Mrs. Bartel collapsed, weeping hysterically. Two police officers led her away. Jessica pressed her hands against her cheeks, too frightened to ask.

Police and fire fighters kept running in and out of the entrance to the stadium in a steady stream. But not until Elizabeth and Jeffrey, with Bruce supported between them, stepped out into the parking lot did a cheer go up from the crowd.

For a moment Jessica couldn't move. All she could do was stare at her sister. Their eyes met across the noisy, milling crowd, and Jessica let out a muffled cry. She pushed herself away from the car and ran into Elizabeth's arms.

"I knew you were in danger," Jessica sobbed. "I knew it. Then Mrs. Bartel came over, and we called the police and came to get you." Tears of relief and happiness ran down her face as she hugged her twin. "I knew—I knew."

Two paramedics led Bruce to the waiting ambulance, and Jeffrey stepped aside to answer questions from the police. Still holding each other tight, Jessica and Elizabeth stood where they were. For a few moments they couldn't speak.

Finally Elizabeth stepped back a pace and looked searchingly into her twin's eyes. "You —knew?"

Jessica nodded. "Yes, I—" She broke off as she remembered *how* she knew. Feeling doubtful and uneasy, she lowered her eyes.

"Jess, how did you know?"

"The Ouija board," she whispered.

Elizabeth sighed, utterly exhausted. "Jess, I know it was all a joke, but this is seri—"

"I swear!" Jessica grabbed Elizabeth's hand. "The board *did* say you were in danger. But remember when you told me that people subconsciously move the planchette to the answers? Well, I kept feeling, I don't know, restless, as though something was wrong. That was *before* Lila and I sat down to ask any questions. And then it showed up on the board that you were in some kind of trouble." Jessica stopped to take a deep breath. "Anyway, you know that you and I always know when the other one is in trouble."

Elizabeth threw her arms around Jessica again. "We do, don't we?" Then she moved back a few steps. "But about that Ouija board—"

Jessica looked down at the ground and whispered, "I'm really, really sorry that Lila and I tricked you. It's all our fault you got into this mess. It never would have happened if we hadn't made up that stuff about Bruce." Two tears trickled down Jessica's cheeks. She had never looked so repentant.

"Promise me one thing, Jess," Elizabeth said softly.

"Sure. What?" Jessica asked, sniffling.

"That you'll never go near a Ouija board again."

"I promise," Jessica said solemnly, then hesitated. "Well, maybe *once* more." She gave her twin a slightly impish smile.

"*Jessica*—" Elizabeth began sternly.

"I mean, just long enough to toss it into the garbage. Even if it *is* Lila's!" Jessica exclaimed.

Laughing, Elizabeth locked arms with Jessica, and together they walked toward the waiting crowd of police.